That's
What's Up!

Also by Paula Chase

SO NOT THE DRAMA

DON'T GET IT TWISTED

That's What's Up!

A Del Rio Bay Novel

PAULA CHASE

Dafina Books

KENSINGTON PUBLISHING CORP.

http://www.kensingtonbooks.com

DAFINA BOOKS are published by

Kensington Publishing Corp.
850 Third Avenue
New York, NY 10022

All Kensington titles, imprints and distributed lines are available at special quantity discounts for bulk purchases for sales promotion, premiums, fund-raising, educational or institutional use.

Special book excerpts or customized printings can also be created to fit specific needs. For details, write or phone the office of the Kensington Special Sales Manager: Kensington Publishing Corp., 850 Third Avenue, New York, NY 10022. Attn. Special Sales Department. Phone: 1-800-221-2647.

Dafina Books and the Dafina logo Reg. U.S. Pat. & TM Off.

ISBN-13: 978-0-7582-2582-5
ISBN-10: 0-7582-2582-2

First Kensington Trade Paperback Printing: July 2008
10 9 8 7 6 5 4 3

Printed in the United States of America

For Ted

"Suck my toe, call me T-E-D"
—Ready Teddy, "The Toe Remix"

Waking the Sleeping Giant

"They hate to see you doing better than them."
—Field Mob ft. Ciara, "So What"

Jessica Johnson glowered.

She stood mannequin-still in the school's long hallway at the floor-to-ceiling glass panes surrounding the fishbowl—the café, Del Rio Bay High's outdoor Beautiful People Only section of the cafeteria. Her eyes, focused like hazel laser beams, glared catlike in her coffee-bean complexioned face.

She couldn't take them off the scene outside.

About forty people milled around the square, no larger than two average-sized bedrooms. Some huddled around the five tall bistro tables—sometimes six people deep. Others stood atop the sandy-colored concrete benches that anchored the corners, while still others were content leaning against one of the two brick walls that enclosed the area. So used to being gawked at from the hall or cafeteria windows, no one paid her much mind. Everyone was enjoying the budding warmth of the early spring—many going jacketless in the fifty-degree Maryland day.

Winter had been short but fierce. Two ice storms had walloped the area, closing school for a total of seven days in February and nearly sending everyone stir crazy from cabin fever. Fifty degrees was almost hot in comparison, the open air addicting.

The thick glass made it impossible for Jess to distinguish any conversations, but she could almost feel the buzz of the various rowdy discussions. Now and then a loud laugh or exclamation would erupt from one of the hubs. Jess assumed it was loud—it had to be if she could hear it from inside. She imagined that the talk was of the Extreme Beach Nationals, the big cheerleading competition taking place in a week, who was heading down to Ocean City with who, which hotel people were staying at and what madness they could get into with their parents lingering nearby.

Typical day in the café, the school's powers discussing who and what was important in DRB High land, in their own version of politicking and strategizing.

The café, twenty feet wide, twenty feet across, and accessible by a single door at the far end of the cafeteria, was nothing more than an island of concrete surrounded by a patch of grass just wide enough to be a pain for the maintenance crew to cut. But it was the students' slice of heaven. No teachers patrolled it. And nobodies stayed away from its door, choosing instead to a) act like the café didn't exist or matter, or b) gaze inside from the windows, like Jess was doing now.

Only she wasn't a nobody. Jess was a café regular, an Upper whose right it was to lounge in the café at her leisure during lunch.

And until that very second, the café had been Jessica's safe haven from wannabes and nobodies, specifically the one wannabe nobody who annoyed her more than anyone in the world . . . Mina Mooney.

Jessica's eyes squeezed into slits, piercing Mina from the shadows of the hall as Mina's head bobbed up and down excitedly, deep in conversation with Kim, the varsity cheer captain, and Sara, Jessica's twin.

Seeing Mina there, all smiles and grins enjoying life in the fishbowl, shouldn't have jolted Jessica. But the flash of heat she felt boiling in her chest was anger—pure and powerful. It grew as she remembered how lightly Sara had mentioned Mina's new "status."

"I was telling Mina that we're gonna kill it at the Extreme," Sara had said, bubbling with a mix of anxiety and excitement at the thought of Nationals.

"Look, I know you two cheer together now, but I'm over hearing you talk about *her*," Jessica snapped. She tossed her hair, a well-kept straight weave that hung just below her shoulders, a ludicrous auburn that almost shimmered next to Jess's dark face, and fixed her twin with a defiant stare.

Sara's light cocoa–complexioned cheeks darkened slightly as the crimson spread through her face. But her voice was neutral as she answered, "I know you guys don't get along." She hesitated for a second then swallowed a sigh before finishing. "Nothing I say will matter, will it? You love to hate Mina."

Jessica laughed, her dark face brightening at Sara's truthful declaration. "Yup. I do."

"Well . . . you know Kim and I invited her to sit in the café, right?" Sara cleared her throat as if admitting it out loud had dried her mouth.

Jessica's smile quickly turned into a sour-lemon scowl and this time Sara's mouth did dry out. Her tongue stuck to the roof of her mouth as she quickly added, "We have a lot of cheer strategy to go over. So you know . . . I mean, you knew Mina was going to get the call to the café eventually, Jess. She's the JV cheer captain . . . she . . ."

"Is a total wannabe, Sara," Jessica huffed. Her finger wagged in Sara's face like she was lecturing a young child, something she did often to her twin when it came to social etiquette. "I know you like hanging out with any and everybody. But Mina is . . . the way she rolls with her . . ." Jessica rolled her eyes and sneered, "clique." She shook her head as if warding off some sort of bad word cooties. "Like they're running things at DRB High." Her next words were thick with venom. "I hate how she thinks her little Miss Nice-Nice act is going to make everyone like her."

Sara giggled, "So let me get this right. You hate her because she's *nice?"* hadn't bothered Jess. She knew that sitting in the café didn't mean much to Sara. Neither did DRB High's whole social hierarchy thing. So it was easy for Sara to dismiss it all as silly or ridiculous. But it wasn't silly to Jess. She rolled with the Glams, the snotty, mostly rich kids, and took her status as a member of the ruling class serious, deadly serious. It hit Jessica where it hurt that Mina—neither rich nor snotty—had always managed to sniggle her way in with the right circles.

Jess had tried, God knows she had, to keep her out. She'd even tried to get her schedule switched around so she'd have the same lunch as Mina this semester, solely to keep Mina on the outside of the fishbowl. None of it made any sense to Sara, who considered Mina a friend. She'd once told Jess, all she wanted was for Jess and Mina to peacefully coexist in the same circles at DRB High.

Peacefully coexist, huh? Jess thought, already nurturing the seed into an idea.

She stared through the thick glass, registering back to the present just as Brian James walked over to the table where Mina sat. He was cute with a capital C, his toffee complexion smooth, eyebrows thick, soft brown eyes accented by thick lashes and a head full of hair so black and curly it made Jess's fingers squirm at the thought of touching it. He stood behind Mina's chair, his six-foot-three frame towering easily over the three-foot high wrought-iron bar chairs, and wrapped his arms around her waist.

Jess averted her eyes from Mina's insanely idiotic grin and focused on Brian. He was telling a joke, she guessed, because all the cheerleaders at the table giggled and Sara gave him a high five. Just as quickly as he came, he whispered something in Mina's ear (more insane teeth-grinding grinning) and sauntered over to a table where a few gaming geeks (award-winning gamers, of course) happily welcomed him into their conversation.

Jess closed her eyes and tried to block out the image of that wide, "I'm such a lucky girl" grin on Mina's face. She tried to force the one word that kept coming up, to describe Mina, back into the far reaches of her mind.

It couldn't be.

Mina was not, could not be . . . an Upper.

No!

True, she was sitting in the café and was dating one of the school's hottest guys. Jess didn't even want to think about Mina's sudden fame as the high-school's "Pop" reporter as people were calling her since she'd snagged the position as writer of her own column, "Pop Life," which showcased the school's up-and-coming stars. Some people were even courting Mina, hoping to get a little ink in "Pop Life."

Blegh!

It was definitely a ridiculous level of freshman beginner's luck. But it didn't make her an Upper, necessarily. Far as Jess was concerned, Mina was popular by association and Jess was being generous by admitting that much.

No, Mina wasn't officially an Upper yet. And if Jessica had anything to do with it, Mina never would be . . . not while they roamed the halls of DRB High together, anyway.

If Mina wanted popularity she'd have to go through Jess first.

Popularity cost, and Jess was going to make sure Mina paid dearly.

"If You Didn't Have That Midterm . . ."

"Into your head, into your mind . . . you can't escape."
—Aly & AJ, "Rush"

Lizzie walked into the Lit class, last of the day, and sat down heavily. She'd never been so happy to get a Friday over with. To get away from classes and the buzzing about spring break. Conversations flew fast and furious as everyone worked to start and finish an entire discussion before the second bell rang.

"What's going on this weekend?"

"Oh my God. The concert last night was sick."

"We're staying at the Xavier down in O.C."

"Dude, that's like a million miles from where everyone else is staying."

The conversations went on like that, weekend plans, spring break plans, weekend, spring break, weekend, spring break.

Lizzie swam silently in the middle of it.

Mina dashed in and immediately joined one of the discussions in progress, no doubt one about the Extreme. Everyone was talking about it. For Lizzie, it was a constant reminder that next week's spring break would be a boring and lonely one.

She slumped in her seat and pulled her Lit notebook from her tote bag. "You too, huh?" she muttered to her bag as, freed of the huge five-subject tablet, it slouched resignedly against her chair.

Empty. *That's exactly how I feel,* she thought.

She wasn't upset about missing the actual competition. Those she could take or leave. But Mina would be gone, their first spring break apart. Because they both stayed ultra busy, holiday breaks had always been their time, sometimes the only time they could hang out without a theater rehearsal or cheer practice interrupting.

Her head bobbed as she heard the name "Todd." She swiveled to see who had said it, but the chatter had already moved on.

It was then that Lizzie faced a truth—she could maybe, possibly have gone this one spring break without her BFF if Todd weren't also heading down to O.C. with JZ, Michael and Brian.

She wasn't sure how it happened, but she'd become one of "those" girls. Somewhere between Mina playing Cupid and Todd getting on one knee, asking her out in only the way Todd could—"Lizzie, would you come with me to the casbah,"—as Rio's Ria crawled with people. Horribly embarrassed by being put on the spot so publicly, but also tickled pink, Lizzie had said yes.

They still joked about the whole "casbah" thing. Todd even set "Rock the Casbah" by The Clash as his ring tone for Lizzie's calls. It was their inside joke.

It felt weird, having an inside joke with a guy who wasn't JZ or Michael.

Wait . . . take it back a step . . . it felt weird having a crush.

Check that, it was a weird crush anyway.

She and Todd's friendship was two parts silly—Lizzie never laughed so much in her life like she did when she was around him—and one part genuine affection. They shared the kind of fragile ease you feel around a person you know well, but are learning to see in a new light.

Some days, he was just the same old crazy Todd she'd known since sixth grade, joking if his mouth was moving, and obsessed with basketball. He had a total dude-crush on JZ, or at least JZ's skill on the hardwood. But other days, Todd was like a stranger. Lizzie hadn't known until recently that he was a complete computer geek. If basketball didn't work out, Todd could seriously do a Bill Gates and start his own tech company. He secretly ran a website called The Joke's on You. The Photoshopped pics of DRB teens mixed in with hot stars looked so real, the site could have been done by a professional.

The site was wildly popular. But no one suspected Todd was the one who had them rolling in celeb circles. He'd revealed his secret to Lizzie two months into their new friendship.

Of course, she'd told Mina one night and swore Mina to secrecy. By week's end the rest of the clique knew. Lizzie spent an entire day in fear that Todd would be mad that she'd told. But he hadn't been. He'd simply sworn them all to secrecy, explaining that anon websites were always way more mysterious and interesting. He liked his anonymous fame. And Lizzie liked that he was a closet techie. It was Todd's geeky side that sealed the crush for her.

"You're more excited that he can code than dunk?" Mina had asked, incredulous.

But Lizzie couldn't help it. That was hot to her. She clamped her hand over her mouth to stifle a spontaneous giggle, then head-checked to see if anyone noticed.

Of course, no one had. People took their time wrapping up their conversations, moving no faster when the bell finally toned the start of class.

Mina took her seat in front of Lizzie and started to say something, when Ms. Qualls launched immediately into an in-depth discussion of *The Grapes of Wrath*. Lizzie scribbled notes furiously. She looked up in time to see a fly buzz through an open window and go straight for the teacher. Ms. Qualls' voice never changed its frantic instructive pitch as she swatted at the curious fly, which insisted on landing on her *Grapes of Wrath* copy.

It occurred to Lizzie that she and the fly were about the only ones paying any attention.

Right as Ms. Qualls attempted to jump-start a discussion on the symbolism of Ma Joad's strength, Lizzie felt Mina's hand tap her calf.

She glanced down, thinking Mina was going to pass her a note, and followed the direction of Mina's jabbing thumb. She frowned down at the ground, wondering what she was looking for, before realizing Mina was pointing toward the door.

Lizzie's breath caught. Todd stood in the hallway grinning, waving and ducking so his body was in the perfect blind spot between Ms. Qualls' classroom entrance and the classroom across from it.

He pulled out his cell phone, typed in something, then nodded to affirm he'd just sent her a message.

Lizzie silently sent praise that her phone was on silent.

She glanced around the comatose classroom, as the teacher droned on.

"What do you think Steinbeck's portrayal of Rose of Sharon is meant to convey?" Ms. Qualls asked.

There was stirring among the students as they shifted, some trying to look more alert. No one volunteered to answer.

Lizzie casually plucked her tote from the floor and flipped her phone open. Her green eyes brightened at the message:

Treat u 2 a slice 2 clbrat end o thtr season?

Lizzie coughed to cover up flipping the phone shut, then dropped her bag back on the floor. As Ms. Qualls gave the class a lackluster lecture about lack of participation, Lizzie gazed slyly over at the hallway, where Todd stood, his arms in a "what's up?" gesture. Students nearest the door openly watched him now, Ms. Qualls' lecture unheard. There was a ripple of head turns as people checked to see who Todd was talking to.

Lizzie nodded slightly and beamed when Todd grinned, gave the thumbs up and disappeared down the hall just as Ms. Qualls glanced to see what had captured the class's attention.

A sliver of thrill tickled Lizzie's neck. Todd had come close to getting caught all for her. He could have sent her the message from the library where he had Independent Study. Instead, he'd risked . . . well, at worst, Todd would have gotten a reprimand from Ms. Qualls who was no stranger to braying at students to get back to class. Still, Lizzie's heart leapt at the sweet gesture.

Her gaze wandered to the hall, hoping for another fleeting glimpse of Todd, but it was empty. Lizzie sighed contentedly and grinned when Mina turned her head long enough to give her a "way to go" wink. She doodled Todd's name in the margins of her notes, joining her fellow classmates in mind-wandering until the bell signaled dismissal.

Now she'd have some *Grapes of Wrath* catching up to do over the break.

Not like she had any other plans, she thought, sulking.

Later that night she walked into the kitchen, stationing herself on a stool across from her mom, who was busy taking a tuna casserole out of the oven. Lizzie sighed, then scowled. She waited a few seconds then sighed louder and scowled harder.

Finally, her mom placed the pan down, slipped off oven mitts and folded her arms. "May I help you?" An ironic smile graced her lips, as if she knew what to expect.

The two of them had played out this scene no less than a dozen times over the last two months. Lizzie played her part accordingly.

"I'm going to be soooo bored over break." She slumped dramatically. Elbows splayed on the countertop, she rested her head on her hand, making sure to keep her eyes on her mom. Before her mom could intone her next line, *Am I crazy? Or would you not be a reluctant tag-along to one of Mina's overnight competitions,* Lizzie rushed ahead. "I know that I've always said the cheer squad gets on my nerves. But that's never stopped me from having Mina's back before."

Lizzie's mom went back to dinner prep. She talked over her shoulder. "Elizabeth, we've gone over this." Plates clattered as she gingerly plucked them from a cabinet. She expertly laid down the plates then moved on to forks. "It's bad enough we have to chauffeur you around for acting classes, auditions and rehearsals. Now you want us to tote you to Mina's stuff too? Not this time, honey," she said, not unkindly, scowling down at the forks in her hand. Lost in thought, she turned them over as if she didn't recognize them, before dumping them in the dishwasher and grabbing several new forks.

Lizzie watched the preparations dispassionately. Normally, she would help out. But she wanted to make sure her mom knew how frustrated she was. She withheld her assistance and waited on the final boom . . .

"If you didn't have that midterm, you could go," her mom said on cue.

End scene, Lizzie thought bitterly.

The conversation was as good as over, now. The fact was, she had an Algebra II exam on the day Mina and her parents were leaving for O.C. And despite Lizzie and Mina's groveling to convince Lizzie's parents to drive her down that Friday, the O'Reillys weren't interested in being in O.C., which would be crawling with fanatic cheer fans and a huge chunk of the Del Rio Bay teen population, thanks to the Extreme falling during spring break.

Marybeth O'Reilly took inventory of the table. With a satisfied cluck, she turned her full attention back to Lizzie. "Me and Dad will plan something with you, if you want." She wriggled her eyebrows, ignoring Lizzie's groan. "We can still be fun."

Lizzie's attempt at a smile, more grimace than grin, fell short.

She pushed herself upright. "That's okay. I have studying to do over break."

"Um-hmm," her mom answered absently. "Go tell Dad dinner's ready."

"I'm not hungry," Lizzie said before skulking off.

Upper A-Go-Go

"Here it goes, here it goes, here it goes again."
—OK Go, "Here It Goes Again"

A huge blue duffel bag sat on Mina's bed, its mouth gaping hungrily, waiting for her to throw more clothes into it. Mina obliged, buzzing about her closet, pulling out every competition necessity—her cheer uni, several pairs of cheer shorts and more spirit tees than she even knew she owned—throwing them toward the bed, mostly missing the bag. Music blared, filling her room, yet the thumping bass was low enough to keep her parents at bay. Her hair, bone straight, hung slightly past her chin, framing her brown-sugar face, and tickled her cheeks as it swung in time to the beat. By the end of the week, her reddish-brown hair would be springy with spiral curls, perfect for pulling into a cute pony for the cheer competition.

Her entire body tingled. It was like the day before Christmas or the night before your birthday, when you know something big is about to happen and all you can think is *Hurry up, tomorrow. Hurry up!*

She'd felt like this ever since being called up to Select Varsity, the new squad Coach Embry had put together in late December.

Mina had already been flying high after her Junior Varsity team placed third at Counties. It was the first time the high school's squad had done that well in three years. Then Varsity had placed fourth. Coach Em immediately came up with the brainchild of creating a competition-only squad of the best members from both squads. Coach Embry's call, the day after Christmas, letting her know she was on the A squad, was Mina's best gift.

Cheerleading had consumed her every thought since.

It apparently never occurred to Coach Em that choosing five out of the eighteen girls from JV would cause hard feelings. Hard feelings nothing—straight up hatred. Kelis, the JV co-captain, for example.

She hadn't made Select and it took the silent, simmering competition that had brewed between her and Mina since their days as recreation cheerleaders to new heights.

Sure, Kelis had given Mina a tight, phony hug in the hall the first time they'd seen each other after the winter break. "Congrats. Hold it down for the fresh fish, girl," she'd said. But after that, their JV practices had been nothing but a string of arguments as they battled over everything from calling cheers at the basketball games to who would lead stretches at practice—things that they'd already battled over during football season.

It had erupted in a final, teary locker-room scene over, of all things, ribbons.

As captain, Mina felt obligated to give each girl an end-of-the-year special gift. The weekend before their last basketball game, she spent an entire day decorating ribbons with each girl's name and graduation year on them. She'd placed each ribbon in its own little box. They were cute, if she could say so herself, and she couldn't wait to hand them out. But somehow, between grabbing her books, the boxes and Brian's basketball hoodie, which he let her wear except on game nights, she'd grabbed only seventeen boxes. And guess whose box was left behind?

Kelis had confronted her angrily and next thing Mina knew the squad surrounded them, instantly separating into the Kelis camp and the Mina camp—the same two camps which had formed months earlier when Kelis had kissed Mina's boyfriend Craig, causing an ugly breakup. But the girls had managed to move past it, Mina for the sake of team unity, Kelis because she never felt truly bad about it in the first place.

It had taken Coach Em walking into the locker room with the box, dropped off by Mina's mom, to cool things off. The circle had quickly dissolved and after that game, the two had barely spoken more than an occasional hey.

Since then, some of the JV girls had threatened not to try out come spring—Kelis among them. But Mina figured, for the girls who really loved cheering (and Kelis was definitely in that mix), being left out would only light the fire and make them work harder to make Select next year—especially if the new squad managed to pull off a win at Nationals.

A win!

It seemed almost impossible. They'd be competing with high schools from all over the East Coast—hot squads from Virginia, New Hampshire and as far west as Ohio—who had been going to the Extreme for years. This was DRB High's first year at the Extreme in five years.

We can't win, Mina thought, even as she daydreamed about doing just that. It would be so hot to win. Nothing gained respect at DRB High like being a part of a winning team. Nothing.

Even as she tried pushing away thoughts of a win at Nationals, she was already thinking about how the Grand Champion jackets that the top team took home would hug her. She wouldn't care if the jacket was made of wool, she'd be sporting it every day into the heat of summer.

She laughed out loud at her own schizzy ways. "I know, I'm tripping, ain't I Chris?" she asked, before blowing a kiss to a huge glossy poster of Chris Brown smiling down at her from the one and only wall her mother allowed her to plaster with posters and miscellaneous cheer memorabilia.

The creamy yellow of the wall was neatly, but totally covered with magazine clippings of the Pretty Ricky/Ne-Yo variety and random photos of her and the clique. She honed in on one in particular.

In it Mina was book-ended by Sara and Kim, who stood in a James Bond pose—fingers steepled mocking a gun, mugging for the camera. The original plan was that she'd hit the Bond pose too, but Brian, who took the picture, made her laugh and instead the camera caught her neck-rolling, fussing good naturedly at him.

That picture was proof she'd made it.

The crowded bistro tables of the café loomed large in the background, just in case anyone questioned where it had been taken.

A National win would be sweet. But as far as Mina was concerned, she'd already taken home the sweetest title—newest member of the Upper clique.

She was in with the senior cheerleaders and no matter how shallow it was, it felt good. It felt even better because she'd earned her invite to the café by putting in work on the cheer floor. No crazy hazing from some Upper or buying somebody a Sidekick for the privilege of sitting in the café, for her.

And the icing on the cake would be three days of bonding at the Extreme with Kim and the other girls on the squad.

If it weren't for her aching arms and legs from two consecutive months of daily two-hour practices (including Saturday), she would swear she was dreaming. She would swear that there was no way that just three months ago, her only hope was to not screw anything up as JV captain before she could make a good impression on the varsity girls—especially Kim.

Now, she spent two hours a day grinding out the routine that Coach Embry hoped would bring Del Rio Bay High their first National Championship, and grumbling side-by-side with the others that Coach Em was totally trying to kill them. Suicide cycles, three straight tumbling passes until your entire body felt limp, for every single imperfect run-through. Coach Em's not-so-subtle way of displaying displeasure.

Mina winced and unconsciously massaged her wrists. She'd lost count of how many suicides they'd done today. She stopped counting at lucky number seven.

Without warning, she abruptly stopped mid-groove, tucked her hair behind an ear and cocked her head toward her desk. A tiny strain of horns played beneath the thumping of the hip-hop coming from her speakers. Mina rushed to the desk. Sitting cross-legged in a swivel chair, she settled in at her computer for a chat, grinning at the waiting message from Lizzie.

Liz-e-O: wad up girlie?
BubbliMi: nuttin . . . packin
Liz-e-O: 4 the Extreme?! It's friggin' like 6 dys awy
BubbliMi: whas ur point? LOL
Liz-e-O: ignore me I'm jus hatin' life since i can't go

Mina's head bobbed in sympathetic understanding. Lizzie had been in a slight funk about missing the Extreme, which tickled Mina since Lizzie's distaste for cheer competitions was legendary. She knew the real reason Lizzie was bummed was tall, had six-pack abs and a moppish head of unruly blonde hair.

Having a similar affliction herself, Mina didn't blame Lizzie for crushing so hard.

Plus, Todd was super cool. Silly almost to the point of being goofy, but in a hot geeky sort of way that made him perfect for the studious, focused Lizzie. They were the classic opposites that attracted, straight out of a *Seventeen* mag quiz.

Mina knew it was killing Lizzie to miss out. If it were her, she'd be climbing the walls right about now, too. She reassured Lizzie, but couldn't help teasing too.

BubbliMi: awww, I'll keep my eye on Todd 4 u

Liz-e-O: What? That's not why I'm mad. I want 2 hang out w/u during spr brk

BubbliMi: w/e Liz. It's ok tht u wanna be w/ur BF

Liz-e-O: so not my bf . . . we're jus friends . . . like good friends

BubbliMi: like friends that kissed, right? ;-)

Mina giggled madly, huddling near her screen waiting to pounce. She imagined Lizzie's face glowing rosy with embarrassment. Lizzie didn't deny the kiss. Instead she came back with a very weak . . .

Liz-e-O: w/e

BubbliMi: OMG Liz, it's ok that u'd rather spend SBk w/him than home w/the rents

Liz-e-O: yeah. It's not just Todd tho. wht am I s'posed 2 do all spring brk w/everybody gone?!

BubbliMi: Cinny and Kelly aren't going

Liz-e-O: true. Still . . . u'll b gone, Mike, JZ

BubbliMi: Todd

Liz-e-O: Grr! Change the channel, please. Seriously, I think me, Cinny & Kelly will be the only three people under the age of 21 left in the DRB next wkend

BubbliMi: I keep telling u 2 ask ur mom if she'll let u ride down w/da guys

Liz-e-O: and I keep telling u ur crazy!! U know they'll say no. God Mi, they barely let me ride w/Brian that night he took us to the mall. A 2 hour road trip?! Fuhgedabowid

BubblMi: LOL I know that's right. Well . . . u, cin and kel get 2 gether and do a girls wkend.

Liz-e-O: not as much fun w/o u

Mina's grin went ear to ear. A pang of best friend love made her heart do a quick step and for a second she felt guilty for looking forward to chilling with the cheer squad. Swiveling in the desk chair, she joked it off.

BubbliMi: so true
Liz-e-O: conceited much?! LOL
BubbliMi: well I know its not da same . . . but at least we're all maxing 2gether sunday.
Liz-e-O: yeah. Thas kewl
BubbliMi: I tell u what, climb in my bag and I'll sneak u down 2 da Xtreme
Liz-e-O: the bad part is, I totally could fit in ur duffel!

Mina's shoulders shook as she howled. She stood up, pushing the chair away with a nudge of her butt.

BubbliMi: c u girl. Gotta finish packing
Liz-e-O: ok l8r

(Un) break•up \ 'brāk-, ə p\
(noun) 1 : an act or instance of breaking up

"I just wonder, do you think of me?"
—Ne-Yo, "Do You?"

Kelly felt like reciting the definition to Angel, but knew it would do no good. She'd been in the "act of" breaking up with him for months now and he still called her regularly, melting her defenses, making it harder and harder for her to stay broken up. She listened intently as he teased, his husky voice accented—a little New York Bronx kick with just enough Puerto Rican accent to make people wonder how long he'd been in America. Laughable, since he hadn't lived in New York since he was five and had never been to Puerto Rico.

"So look, girl, stop playing games with me."

As usual, Kelly was glued to the phone, anxious and excited by Angel's prodding. She especially loved how sometimes they'd switch from speaking English to Spanish. As if they were really hiding their conversation from anybody.

Everyone in Kelly's household spoke fluent Spanish—always had. Her grandfather was a first-generation Puerto Rican immigrant. He'd worked himself into the high ranks of corporate America by blending in, but when he was home they spoke Spanish. Always.

He'd been dead five years now. But still, Spanish was the first language in the Lopez household.

Just then Angel did it, nearly whispering in Spanish, "You know I'm feeling you, baby girl. Give me a chance."

Kelly sighed, closing her eyes. She loved the velvet edge Spanish gave Angel's voice. But she wouldn't let herself be pulled in by Mr. Romantic. Because somewhere behind him always came the trash talker.

"Angel, you know I can't," Kelly forced herself to say. Her fingers flitted, moving the same piece of chestnut colored hair behind her ear, pulling it out only to tuck it again.

"Naw. You *can*," Angel said, his voice louder but not yet angry. "You won't, you mean."

"Okay, then I won't," Kelly said softly in Spanish, switching because sometimes speaking it calmed her. She ignored the anxiety gnawing away at her confidence and dove in, in English. "But you're just as guilty too."

"Me?" His voice came back genuinely surprised.

"Yes. You say you can't give up the game . . . but I think it's that you won't."

Kelly heard his sigh come out in a loud, long exhale. She could hear the unspoken, *we've gone over this a million times*. She tried to smooth over the tension that could be felt even through the phone.

"I'm fine being friends, Angel. I . . ."

"Naw, you fine with me chasing you," he blasted back. Anger deepened his accent.

"How am I making you chase me?" Kelly asked, her surprise genuine.

"Man, forget this," Angel said. And Kelly could almost hear him pacing as he began cursing in Spanish. He went on for a few seconds then seemed to realize he was still on the phone. He came back, in English. "Your ass ain't all that."

The words stung Kelly but they also made her angry. "Maybe. But who's been after who for the last four months?"

And incredibly, Angel hung up on her.

For a second, Kelly thought it was a dropped call. She called his name a few times to make sure he wasn't still out there stunned into silence by her strong response.

But no, he'd definitely hung up. She knew for sure when her phone didn't ring seconds later with the customary dropped-call dance of apologies. She sat, the Sidekick beside her, in case he called back, and had been staring at the phone a full seven minutes before she realized she wanted it to ring back.

Okay, so a part of me enjoys him chasing me, she admitted to herself.

What she didn't enjoy was Angel acting as if him selling drugs wasn't a big deal. Kelly had already lied by omission to her grandmother. As far as Grand was concerned Angel was a nice, if not unfortunate, young man. Lying was one thing, continuing the lie was another and Kelly drew the line there. She couldn't date Angel knowing that huge lie was out there.

What if she were with Angel and he got busted? A nightmare her grandmother had already lived with Kelly's parents.

I'm definitely not my mother, Kelly thought, snorting in derision at flashes of her mom's retelling of how she and Kelly's dad, a drug dealer, now behind bars, had gotten together.

She picked up the Sidekick. Her fingers ached to call Angel back. But her mind clamped shut against the idea, remembering vividly Jacinta calling her and Angel the ghetto version of *Beauty and the Beast*.

"Y'all are just too different," Jacinta had said dismissively.

Kelly agreed that they were like *Beauty and the Beast*, but not in the sarcastic way Jacinta meant it.

The whole point of *Beauty and the Beast* was that the Beast had a sincere heart under his growl. Kelly thought Angel did too. If she hadn't, things would have been totally over, after the disastrous party he and Raheem had before the Christmas break, instead of this perpetual act of breaking up.

Just then the phone rang and Kelly dropped it as if bitten. She laughed at herself, grinning harder when she saw Angel's number.

"You hung up on me," she said, doing a poor job of sounding mad.

Angel's voice was hushed and serious. "Yeah. I'm sorry. Kelly look . . ." There was a long pause. Kelly frowned down at the phone, wondering if the connection had been lost.

Angel's voice came back, stronger but no louder. "I never asked you to agree with what I do. Have I?"

Kelly answered uncertainly. "No."

"I don't see why it's always gotta be between us. But . . ."

"Because, I told you about my father and—"

Angel cut her off. "I know. But I'm not your pops." He rushed on. "Look, we had this discussion already." Kelly nodded in agreement as he continued. "I ain't call to talk that yang again. I'm saying, I respect that you did what you had to, breaking it off. But I'm feeling you and if you trying give me a second chance, I'll do right."

Kelly zoned in on a spot on the wall, narrowing her eyes at it, as if it had spoken the words instead of Angel. Her heart pounded in her ear through the phone.

"You hear me?" Angel asked.

"Are you saying you're . . . that you . . ."

"Getting out the game? Yeah," Angel said flatly. He met Kelly's long silence with a chuckle. "All this time you been wanting this and now you don't have nothing to say?"

"Well, how are you going to get out?" Kelly whispered.

"You don't need worry about all that," Angel said tersely. His voice softened immediately. "Your turn to answer me. You with me, once it's done?"

Kelly nodded, prompting Angel to prod, "You not leaving me hanging, are you?"

"Oh, no. I was nodding I . . ." Kelly giggled. "Yes. I'm with you."

Kelly heard the smile as he said in Spanish, "That's my girl."

FWBs

"Can somebody help me, help me get out of this circle."
—Marques Houston, "Circle"

Raheem's voice came out of the darkness. "You letting your hair grow long, huh?"

He and Jacinta sat side by side on his bed, only inches apart. But it was too dark for her to see his face, to gauge if there was anything hidden in the question. In her mind's eye Jacinta could see his thick eyebrows relaxed, a small grin playing on his lips to match what sounded like a good mood. Tufts of hair from his frayed braids, in need of freshening up, wisping around his hairline, making him look like he'd just swiped a hat off his head.

That was the Raheem she'd known forever—best friend turned boyfriend—except now with a twist, because he was her ex. As in broken up, kaput since December.

If he'd asked her that question before they'd broken up she would know how to answer. But she wasn't sure how to answer ex-boyfriend.

It was a simple enough question. And the answer was obvious—yes, she was letting her hair grow out.

She'd worn her hair short for the last two years. But after she and Raheem broke up over the Christmas holiday, she'd decided to try something different. It had been rough going at first—going from short to long always is. The clique had teased her daily when the sides of her hair went from a slick curl to a thick poof. Now she was finally over the puffy stage. Her dyed blonde hair was now a cute mid-length curly shag, which framed her honey-golden face perfectly. She was now toying with letting it go back to its natural sandy brown color.

Yes, I'm growing it out. Changing my style to go along with my new status as Cinny without Raheem, she thought silently in the quiet darkness.

Yet, she still hadn't answered aloud. Because as obvious as it was that she was letting her hair grow out, as conversationally and calmly as he'd asked it, the question coming from ex-boyfriend, Raheem— her friend with benefits, as Jacinta preferred to think of him—could easily be a booby trap. Now it was an easygoing convo about her new 'do, but in a few minutes it would probably be an angry disagreement, ending with Raheem saying that her hair change was just another in a million other changes Jacinta had made since moving in with her Aunt Jacqi in The Woods. Another sign that she "thought she was cute" and was turning into "one of those gray chicks from DRB High."

It was so stupid to worry about how to answer such an ordinary question. She had to say something, so she muttered, "Um-huh," keeping the answer neutral.

"It's cute," Raheem said. His fingers caressed her thick curls gently.

Jacinta clenched her jaw against a sigh of relief and regret. She shouldn't be here. She and Raheem were broken up. If anyone had walked in on them ten minutes ago, they wouldn't have been able to tell, though.

Her stomach rolled over. *Why do I keep doing this?* she thought, staring bleakly at the ceiling. *Boredom? Loneliness? Burn-out from spending all of Friday night and half of that day gaming with her younger siblings?*

Whatever it was, every other weekend, when she went back home it never failed to show up. She'd be all set to sit in the house the entire weekend and then Angel would call. It was always Angel, never Raheem. And the conversation always went the same. It had become their new friendship ritual—the way things were now that she and Raheem were FWBs.

"What you doing, girl? Want hang out?" Angel would say.

Jacinta would hem and haw, think about the alternative—spending the entire weekend playing video games with her brothers and sister—something she enjoyed but not for two days straight. Then she'd think about the inevitable argument she and Raheem would have over something stupid and begin to say, "Naw, I catch y'all later." Then Raheem's voice would float from the background, nonchalant, smooth and chocolate, "Tell her come on and stop playing. She know she want roll."

Hearing his voice always did it. It wasn't planned. Every time she came home, back to Pirates Cove, she swore she'd say no this time.

And yet, here she was. She felt sick about being so weak, so unable to break the habit of spending her weekends with Raheem and Angel. It had been second nature most of her life. They'd been friends since she was five years old. It had never occurred to her what life would be like if they weren't going out. Now she knew.

"Why you so quiet?" Raheem asked. He scooted over so they were hip to hip.

Jacinta took a deep breath. Her chest was tense but she knew she had to say it. "Heem . . . you know we . . . it's not like we're back together, because . . . just 'cause we're hooking up."

He sucked his teeth and Jacinta felt his thigh tense beside her as he said, "Yeah Cinny, you say that every single time."

Jacinta winced. "You act like it happens all the time."

Raheem snorted. "Hasn't it?"

Jacinta thought back on it. *Four months, seven weekends . . .*

"It hasn't been *every* weekend," she said weakly, unable to come back with anything as Raheem blew out a long breath.

His voice edged closer to argument territory. "Whatever, Cinny. While we getting facts straight, the reason we're not back together is 'cause you keep throwing shade."

Jacinta shook her head in the darkness as she corrected him. "No, I never said no I don't want to get back together. When you ask what's up with us, I ask if you gon' stop tripping about me and what I'm doing when I'm home."

"Home?" Raheem interrupted. "So The Woods home now?"

Jacinta heard the smirk in his question. *I knew it,* she thought to herself. From talking about her hair to this.

She inhaled deeply then let it out quietly, slowly through her nose, before responding. "Whatever, Heem. You know what I mean. Over my aunt's. And this is why we not officially back together." She snorted. "I'm surprised you haven't moved on anyway. What happened to . . . whatever her name is who you was all up on in December?"

Raheem's silence was thick in the darkness.

Jacinta sucked her teeth. "We argue just as much apart as we do together."

"Not like I'm twisting your arm when you come home," Raheem said, a nasty sneer in his voice.

This time, Jacinta didn't give him the satisfaction of answering, mainly because he was right.

I can't keep doing this, she muttered to herself.

Her and Raheem needed to be together or apart because this halfway thing was worse than the arguing that led to the breakup and the heartbreak she felt when they first split.

But it wasn't that simple. When she was in Pirates Cove, she wanted to be with Raheem, wanted things to be like before. But when she was back in The Woods, seven miles away, she loved her freedom. Out of sight, out of mind was no joke—it was exactly how she felt about him when she was back at Aunt Jacqi's where her father had sent her to live eight months ago.

She dreaded spring break. Her aunt was going away on a business trip to New York. Weekends were hard enough. What was she going to do back in Pirates Cove Thursday through Sunday?

She pushed herself off the bed, ready to head home. Standing in the darkness, she wondered what else to say.

She'd already asked her father if he could take her back to Aunt Jacqi's early (home, whether Raheem liked it or not). She couldn't wait to get back to the 'burb side of the DRB Bridge. That seven miles between her and Raheem kept her honest. Once there, she didn't have the same flood of emotion, the struggle to keep herself away from Raheem, away from the hope that if he tried harder they could make their relationship work.

Her phone buzzed and Jacinta looked down at the message from Mina:

da click iz chilln 2mrw @ mikes 2:00. u b bk hm?

The words calmed her.

The clique was hooking up tomorrow. Just what she needed to wash this weekend off her. The confusion and uneasiness she felt about hooking up with Raheem without them being an actual couple almost always disappeared once she was tripping and dissing with the clique.

Her mood lifted. "Alright, well I talk to you later," she said to Raheem.

Raheem reached out, meaning to grab her hand. But his hand grazed her belly. If it had been like old times, Jacinta would have automatically gone to him to cuddle.

This time she stood stock still and he had to pull her gently back over to him. "How we gon' talk later if you don't call me?" he asked.

"I meant I guess we'll catch up later . . . you know, when I come home Thursday," Jacinta said, anxious to go.

The dark room was suffocating even though Raheem was being sweet now. When he was sweet it was hard for Jacinta to keep her attitude. She still loved him. A fact she didn't so much deny as try to resist.

Resist, because she was sick of bickering about the same old stuff—
he didn't get to see her enough, who was that in the background talking when he called her, where was she. He criticized or questioned
everything she did and said, since she'd moved to The Woods.

"So you not gon' call me?" Raheem prodded.

"You can call me, you know," Jacinta teased, her mind on texting
Mina back.

"Yeah, but when I do you usually busy with your . . . clique." He
said the last word like it hurt him. "I may as well just wait for you to
call . . . you know, when you got time for me."

When Jacinta answered she was careful not to sound too pouty,
too mad, too anything. "Anytime you call I talk to you, Raheem.
Don't make it like I be blowing you off."

"I didn't say that," he said innocently.

Always the games, she thought.

The silence grew around them for a few minutes before she finally got up the nerve to exit again. "Alright, well . . . I better go."

"It's like that? No kiss or nothing?" Raheem asked, pretending to
pout, wanting her to believe he was playing around, uncaring about
getting a kiss. But Jacinta heard real hurt in his voice and it tugged at
her heart. Raheem wasn't the sensitive type.

She bent down to kiss him and they bumped foreheads. She giggled. "Sorry."

He pulled her down on his lap and guided her face to his. They
kissed and the usual heat she felt when they were that close was
there, not raging, but definitely there. When Raheem's hands began
to rub Jacinta's back she popped up hastily.

"Alright, Heem. See you."

"Alright," he said sullenly.

Jacinta stood by him for a second, waiting for him to stand up
and walk her to the door. But he didn't.

She straightened her back and headed out.

Tomorrow couldn't come fast enough.

Sunday Clique'n

"Turn around and bless me with your beauty."
—Bobby Valentine, "Slow Down"

Lizzie's legs, long and slender, went on for days. Especially in the canary yellow pants with fine gray pinstripes.

Mina never understood how someone with legs as long as Lizzie's wasn't considered tall. But Lizzie wasn't. She was only an inch or so taller than five-foot Mina. But where Mina had curves and muscles, Lizzie was thin, not quite shapeless but definitely unassuming, until she wore an outfit that accented her slim waist and slender-hipped legginess. It was a shape perfect for modeling because everything fell just right on her. So Michael said, constantly.

As Michael's creations for the school's theater productions became more and more everyday wearable, Mina had once whined, "How come you never want me to model?" Michael seriously had some outfits that she'd sport in public in a heartbeat.

In answer, he'd merely dismissed her with a tap to her athletic buns.

Standing alongside Kelly, Mina admired yet another Michael James masterpiece.

Michael fluttered about Lizzie, busily pinning the pants leg, tugging at the waist and generally fussing the costume, a 1930s-style man suit, into perfection. The pants, pleated in front, hung loosely on Lizzie's long-legged frame, ending in a more precise fit at the ankle. Under normal circumstances Mina would have laughed out loud at the notion that she'd like a pair of bright yellow pants. With pinstripes, no less.

But she marveled, mouth agape, at how even with the pinstripes it was easily an outfit that would get compliments. It was hot.

Michael had done it again—given a retro outfit a funky update. It was, in Michael's own words, a modern day zoot suit (swearing he'd made up the term, Mina had to Google it) with a definite hip edge.

Lizzie fiddled with the suspenders, another risky fashion choice that Michael had made work, careful not to move an inch where Michael's hands danced around her legs. Her arms glowed tan against the stark white sleeveless tee that fit snug around the low waist of the pants. She rattled on, already talking about the summer production and possibly trying out for The Players, Del Rio Bay's premier theater production company, now that Michael had an in and was doing costuming for them.

Mentally sizing up whether she'd look as good as Lizzie in the pants (probably not), Mina turned to ask Cinny what she thought and stopped mid-inhale at the cozy scene across the room.

JZ and Jacinta were playing pool.

If pool consisted mostly of Jacinta scratching up Michael's pool table with her choppy attempts, and JZ staring squarely at Jacinta's lush backside wiggling in the air each time she bent over to take a shot.

"Okay, Cinny. Can you at least pretend to know what you're doing?" JZ cracked. He shook his head at yet another pitiful attempt by Cinny to whack the ball with her cue stick.

She waved him off and bent back over. JZ's eyes followed her butt like a magnet to a refrigerator, openly ogling.

Mina cleared her throat in an exaggerated "ahem," but she was too far away for them to hear.

JZ and Jacinta had been awfully cozy the last few weeks, openly flirting but pretending it was dissing.

They weren't fooling anybody. Something was popping off and Mina had made it clear, in a very nice way of course, that she thought it wasn't such a good idea. She'd casually reminded Jacinta how many girls JZ had already gone out with since the school year started.

"Girl, who you telling," Jacinta had laughed. "I think he's trying to break a record."

"You must be trying to be girl number fifteen," Mina had joked. But the way she'd looked at Jacinta provided the unspoken, *are you?*

"Hell to the naw," Jacinta had said, cracking them both up again. "You know Jay my buddy." She'd shoved Mina's shoulder. "Don't worry. I'm not gonna put you in the middle like I am with Angel and Kelly."

Mina had felt a ridiculous amount of relief. It probably showed on her face and she was almost embarrassed. It was selfish to begrudge Jacinta a little fun. After her very public breakup with Raheem, whether it was JZ or Justin Timberlake, Jacinta deserved to enjoy a little playing the field.

There was a lot Mina hadn't said, that day. She knew she didn't have to. Jacinta knew exactly how Mina was feeling. The back and forth between Angel and Kelly had been a thorn in Jacinta's side for months. Known for speaking her mind, she'd admitted it many times to Mina, to Kelly and anyone else who would listen.

Still, Mina felt bad for being such a bulldog about the no-flirting-with-friends rule. She wanted to not care. Let JZ and Jacinta have their fun.

Jacinta knew JZ was a player. And she was way savvier about guys and relationships than Mina would ever be. But whenever they got too cozy, alarms rang in Mina's head.

Jacinta's ex was one of JZ's chief rivals on the hardwood and in football. Mina knew the last thing JZ would ever do is give an opponent fuel in the game, especially not over a girl. Still she wondered if JZ saw flirting with Jacinta as another competition with Raheem. That's what worried her.

Nothing good could come of JZ and Jacinta's increasingly affectionate "playing."

After carefully positioning herself for what seemed to Mina a good five minutes, confirming for Mina that Cinny knew JZ was watching her (and liking it), Jacinta's stick still scratched more table than it did ball. JZ sucked his teeth. But even from across the room, Mina knew he wasn't nearly as annoyed as he was making out.

"Seriously?" JZ exclaimed as the ball Jacinta was aiming for stood stock still. She hadn't even come close enough to stir up a breeze near it. "Raheem never showed you how to play pool?" He raised his voice loud enough to be heard on the other side of the room. "You're as bad as Mina."

"Whatev, Jay," Mina hollered back.

JZ stood behind Jacinta, positioning her arms. "Look, I'm down with winning, but you're not even competition. Come on, girl." He bent over Jacinta, imitating the proper stance, forcing her body to mock his. "You're not putting enough force on the right end of the stick."

The two of them stood locked in the pose until Jacinta hit the ball to his satisfaction. JZ lingered—a second too long—as they watched the stick connect with the green ball, sending it rolling slowly a few inches away.

Okay, playtime over, Mina thought.

Just as Michael asked, "What do you think, Diva?" she left the conversation abruptly and strode over to the pool table.

"Umm . . . what's all *this*?" Mina gestured grandly to JZ and Jacinta before folding her arms in mock disapproval.

"What?" JZ said, but his smile was crooked and pooched at the same time, in that "caught" kind of way. "Why you rummin'?"

Mina squinted. "Why am I what?"

"Oh, y'all don't know nothing 'bout that," JZ yelled, teasing. "That's that new hotness I just made up. Rummin', it means tripping."

"That word is not hot," Mina snorted.

"Alright, don't let me find out later that you jocked my word," JZ said.

"Yeah, whatever." Mina nodded her head toward Jacinta. "What's going on with y'all, all buddy-buddy?"

Jacinta laughed. "Uh-oh, the Princess is suspicious."

"Man, I'm just trying get a real game going on here," JZ said. Reluctantly, he put more distance between him and Jacinta. He and Mina had an unspoken thing about him scoping out her girlfriends. She hated when he did it—so he tried not to do it in front of her.

"What's the rule, Princess? JZ not allowed to mack on anyone in the . . ." Jacinta took an exaggerated bow, her hands together. "Inner circle."

Mina pointed at JZ, a silent "you know better" passing between them.

A huge grin spread over JZ's face as he yelled, "Ay! Man, I'm glad you're here."

He laughed, loud and hard, at Mina's confused look.

Brian came up behind Mina and wrapped his arms around her, teasing. "You stirring up trouble, toughie?" He threw up a fist in a "what's up" in Michael's direction.

There were murmurs of "hey" and "what's up" from Kelly, Lizzie and Michael.

As if Brian's voice and touch flicked a No Nagging switch in her head, Mina immediately went soft and flirty.

"Hey." She giggled. "Now when do I ever cause trouble?"

That set the whole clique laughing.

"Y'all are so wrong," Mina said, a small grin dancing at the corner of her mouth.

JZ took a quick shot at the striped yellow ball, barely taking aim, and sent it flying to the corner pocket as he tattled, "Your girl all up in my bidness."

"No, that's you and Cinny all up in each other's business," Mina said, enjoying the way she and Brian rocked slowly back and forth in his strong warm bear hug. She never tired of him holding her like that.

"You gotta give it to him, Mi. He did wait till she was boyfriend-less," Michael quipped. He stood upright, finally finished hemming one of Lizzie's pants legs, and surveyed his work.

"That's right, boyfriend LESS," Jacinta chirped.

Mina listened for any sadness in the proclamation. For weeks Jacinta had been in a bad way about her and Raheem's breakup. But just recently, around the same time she and JZ's flirting was on the up tick, she seemed to really be over Raheem. If there was such a thing.

Mina had a feeling Cinny simply had good and bad days. Today must have been a good one because there was nothing but happiness in her voice.

Mina was glad. A little wary maybe, that a little canoodling masked as a pool lesson was a classic JZ mack move . . . but Brian smelled good (sporty rustic) and felt good (strong, athletic arms). She had better things to do than fuss with JZ.

Still, she couldn't resist one last parting shot. "You go ahead messing with Cinny." Mina stuck her leg out and took a swipe with her foot at JZ's ankle, as far as she could without leaving the comfort of Brian's arms. "You're gonna be hurting when she goes running back to Raheem."

"Man, she can run, walk or sprint, that's her business," JZ bragged.

Jacinta snorted. "Who? How about none of the above?" She arched her right eyebrow and shot Mina a look. "Me and Raheem are finished. O-V-E-R."

"Uhh . . . that doesn't spell finished," Lizzie pointed out from across the room. Michael gave Lizzie's pants a light tug, dismissing her from the stand.

She stepped down and went behind a large rice-paper screen to change back into her regular clothes. Michael busied himself tidying up the corner of pins, swatches and miscellaneous costuming tools, only partially tuned in to the conversation as the clique did what they did best, give one another a hard time in the name of friendship.

Jacinta turned back to the pool table. Sizing up a ball, she bent over, fixed her body the way JZ had shown her, and tapped the ball just enough for it to rock.

She took a silly curtsy as JZ clapped daintily, his kudos small like her accomplishment. Grinning, she picked up where she left off in the conversation. "Naw, me and Raheem are done like the Thanksgiving Day turkey."

"Um-huh," Mina said, openly skeptical. "Like I said, JZ, don't come crying to me when your flirt buddy all hugged up with her man."

JZ made a face like "as if," then took one last shot. He sat down on the corner of the pool table, his long legs splayed in front of him, the game forgotten. "So we're still on for the Extreme, right?" he asked Brian, rubbing his hands together at the thought of the road trip. "Your moms still cool letting us stay at y'all condo?"

"Yeah." Brian tickled Mina's side, then walked to the corner to get a pool stick. "Everybody knows they're on their own with grub though, right? I'm not gonna be cooking for a bunch of hard heads. And respect my crib or else my people's gonna be all over me about responsibility blah, blah, blah."

He nudged Jacinta out of the way gently and racked up the balls.

She took a seat next to JZ on the pool table. Her feet, dangling two feet from the floor, kicked lightly.

"Man, as long the honeys in full effect, I'll eat project noodles everyday," JZ said. "I'll pack a few extra packets and bring my secret ingredient."

Lizzie made her way over and pulled up a stool next to where Mina stood. "Jay, you're such a gourmet," she snickered.

Kelly brought over a bar stool for herself and one for Mina. The three of them stationed themselves just far enough from the pool table so they wouldn't be knocked out with a pool stick.

"Yeah, grated parmesan cheese and ramen noodles is so five star," Mina said, hopping onto the stool. She nearly fell off, kicking at JZ's stick poking at her feet.

"Whatever," JZ said. "I don't care what we eat as long as we rolling with some shorties."

Mina was constantly perplexed by her male friends' endless freedom. For the millionth time she griped aloud about it. "Why do boys always get to do whatever they want?"

"Brian, your mom isn't worried about you being on your own for two days?" Kelly asked.

"Well I'm potty trained and my address is sewn into all my shirts, in case I get lost," Brian said, leaning into his shot.

The clique's laughter was a motley chorus of the boys' choppy, coarse guffaws and the girls' musical giggling.

Kelly ignored his sarcasm. "I just meant . . . your parents really trust you. We have a condo in O.C. too. But I can't see my grandmother letting me go down there solo before I'm eighteen."

Mina chimed in, agreeing. "My parents have rules from here to L.A. The only way they'd let me stay somewhere with no chaperones is if there were nanny cams hidden in the condo everywhere."

"That's y'all little boogee, sheltered girls," Jacinta said. She crossed her legs primly as she boasted, "My father not *that* strict."

"But would he let you go to O.C. and stay with the guys?" Kelly challenged.

The girls stared her down. Jacinta had more freedom than any of them, but none of them believed she had that much.

Jacinta's eyebrows worked, rising and falling as she thought about it. Finally she answered, "Yeah, I think he would."

There was a collective, "yeah, right" eye roll from Mina, Lizzie and Kelly.

"That's my kind of pops," JZ said. He and Brian exchanged a pound and a boys' locker room snicker.

"Cinny, I don't believe that," Mina said.

"Maybe not with JZ and Brian, because he doesn't know them," Jacinta said. "But I think he'd let me go with Raheem and Angel."

"Your dad is way more liberal than my parents, then," Lizzie said.

"No, that's not it," Jacinta said. She schooled the girls in her worldly, I've-seen-things-you'll-never-experience voice, a mix of genuine sharing and light superiority. "My father already knows me and Raheem have sex. So, what's the point of him not letting me go? The ship has sailed."

The girls were quiet as they considered this. But the guys had a field day with it.

"Like I said, my kind of pops," JZ crowed again. He and Brian went for the double fist pound and handshake on that one.

Still skeptical, Mina shook her head in disbelief. "Wait . . . Cinny, just because he knows y'all get down like that doesn't mean he's gonna send you off for a whole weekend to do what you want."

"Alright, I'm not saying he gonna be like 'yeah whatever,'" Jacinta admitted. She spoke matter-of-factly. "Real talk, the only reason your parents have all those rules is to prevent the inevitable."

Lizzie scowled. "Having sex isn't inevitable."

Jacinta laughed. "Lizzie, you're like the poster child for innocence. Not everybody is into your fifteenth-century dating method, where you hold hands at the six month mark and kiss for the first time at a year."

"First of all, it's seventeenth century," Lizzie said, taking the teasing in stride. It was no secret she believed in taking things slow. She wasn't embarrassed by it and proved it by poking fun at herself. "And second of all, hand holding is allowed at the two month mark."

Kelly and Mina laughed. But Mina's laugh was hollow. She and

Brian were stuck somewhere between Lizzie's slow burn relationship style and Mina's own desire to let the relationship go at its own
pace. They were well past hand-holding and pecking on the lips, but
nowhere near the "inevitable."

It wasn't something she and Brian had discussed and she wasn't
about to have their first conversation about it be in a group. She
steered the conversation back to Jacinta's theory. "Alright, so you're
saying that once your father found out about you and Raheem he
let you do what you wanted? No curfew? Nothing like that?"

"No. I still have a curfew when I'm home but he stopped trying
to plan every second of my day. Because he knew . . ." Jacinta paused
for a second then shrugged. "All the rules in the world not gonna
stop it, if it's gonna happen." She chuckled dryly. "And once it does,
what are the rules stopping?"

Mina considered that. She wanted to ask Jacinta how her dad had
found out. What had happened? What did he say?

The thought of having that kind of conversation with her father
made her queasy. Her father was generally the good cop, compared
to Mina's mom's hardnose inquisitions. But talking about sex with
him? No thanks.

"All I know is, it sucks that you guys can go and we can't," Lizzie
said.

"And all I know is, it's gon' be wi-iild," JZ hooted. "All those
cheer shorties running around in their teeny skirts." A tiny smile on
his face, he shook his head like someone who'd just had a very pleasant vision of the future. He called over to Michael, "Son, we gon'
have a blast."

Michael took his time putting away the last of his pins before
walking over to the pool table. "Ay, kid, I may not go," he said finally,
nonchalant.

JZ frowned. He and Mina both sang, "Why?"

"Okay wait," Lizzie said. Her face took on a chiseled frown as if
she were trying to solve a complex equation. "So me, Kelly and Ja-

cinta want to go and can't . . . and Michael, you're *not* going now? Did I hear you right?"

Michael shrugged it off. All eyes were on him but he pretended to be engrossed in some fuzz on the pool table. He picked at it as he spoke. "Ms. Jessamay doing some costume work for The Players and asked if I would help out."

"For real?" JZ asked, in a strange high-pitched voice, as if Michael had just said he was heading to Mars for spring break.

Mina picked up on the flicker of frustration in JZ's face. Michael's costume work was still an awkward topic for him. Michael's drawing skills had always been fire. But once Michael had begun using those skills to draw outfits, JZ hadn't figured out how to take all the costume sketches, fittings and talk of how an outfit "fell" on somebody. He blocked it out anytime the conversation turned to it. And normally anytime the clique got together, he always piped in first, volunteering his house—Mina assumed, to avoid coming to Michael's, since half of what used to be Michael's basement bedroom manpartment was now what JZ called a dress shop.

"The only thing Michael missing in that corner of the room is one of those fashion dummies," he'd told Mina, his mouth upturned.

Mina hadn't bothered to lecture him on how foul his attitude was. She and JZ sparred about it constantly but his stance on the topic hadn't changed for the better yet.

JZ regained his air of playful dissing. "I mean . . . I'm not knocking your hustle, playah. That's more shorties for me."

The answer seemed to relieve Michael because he came over, his fist out for a pound.

"Yeah, I figured that," Michael said as he and JZ banged fists.

"So what are *we* supposed to do over break?" Lizzie asked glumly.

"I say you, Kelly and Cinny cool out together," Mina said. She saw Lizzie's green eyes deaden to a dull jade at the suggestion and quickly tried to help them plan a grand spring break. "Do a spa day on Thursday. And then Friday, go to the movies. You know that one with Nick Cannon comes out that day." She huffed a little. "I really wanted to see it too."

Lizzie huffed, "Oh my God. Do not act like your missing some Nick Cannon movie is the same as us having to stay home like the ugly stepsisters from the ball."

"Who?" Jacinta scowled. She put her hands on her hips. "Maybe you and Kelly are ugly stepsisters, but not me."

"Hey, me either," Kelly said.

The girls joked back and forth about who got to be Cinderella.

With the tension eased some, Mina brought up the Extreme again.

"Jay, don't go thinking just because Brian is driving you're gonna have him all over O.C. cruising for chicken heads."

JZ palmed her face. "Yeah, yeah."

Mina pushed his hand away, lecturing on. "I'm serious. Y'all are planning to be at the competition . . ." She arched an eyebrow, high. "Right, Brian?"

"Yes, dear," Brian joked, never looking up from the pool table.

"Aw dag, he yes-deared you," JZ howled. "You know that's code word for, *girl please, I'm gonna do what I want when I get there.*"

"It better not be," Mina said, giving Brian a look.

He looked up from the table and winked at her, dissolving her scowl into a smile. She stuck her tongue out at JZ.

"See, that's why I was hoping Money Mike was going." JZ sucked his teeth. "Todd and Brian ain't gonna be no fun since they have *girlfriends.*"

He said it like it was a four-letter word.

At the mention of Todd's name connected with the word "girlfriend," Lizzie grinned but quickly hid it when Mina looked her way.

"What?" she asked, at Mina's wide, cat-ate-the-canary smile.

Mina shook her head and went back to her ground rules for the

Extreme. "Friday night is the Individuals and partner stunt event. So y'all meet me there at the convention center."

JZ scowled. "Wait. Why do we need to sit at the events you're not even in?"

Michael laughed. "Sure you don't want stay home with me, kid?"

"Man, for real." JZ rolled his eyes.

"Jay, come on," Mina pleaded. "How else you gonna meet girls if you're not at the events?"

JZ thought about it for a second but didn't get a chance to answer.

"Exactly. So okay, Individuals on Friday," Mina said.

She rattled on, laying out the entire weekend, letting them know when and what time the guys could hook up with her or with her and the Blue Devils squad, ignoring the clique as they teased JZ.

The look of irritation on JZ's face as his entire spring break was planned to the second was a mild victory for the ones being left behind.

Total BFF Control

"Another day, another drama."
—Britney Spears, "Piece of Me"

Across town in Kelly's posh nabe, Folgers Way, Jessica sat in Mari-Beth Linton's grand, pimped-out bedroom. She was so sure and confident about her plan, she'd been excitedly rambling on about it for the last ten minutes, oblivious to the scowl creeping across Mari-Beth's face.

It rattled Jessica when Mari-Beth looked up from giving herself a pedi and blurted icily, "I don't get it. Why do you care?" She swung her lush, blonde hair to the side, rested her chin on her knee and reached for her toes with the polish brush. She frowned. "Shoot, I smudged it. Jess, can you come do this for me?"

Her hand was already outstretched, thrusting the bottle of pink dazzle polish Jess's way.

Jess looked down at her own still-wet toes.

Now my toes will be a hot mess, Jess thought, clenching her teeth against the sigh building in her chest.

For a second she considered saying no or at least, "wait a minute"—but only for a second before she walked over to the window seat where Mari-Beth sat. Jess surveyed the emerald green, perfectly manicured lawn beyond the window. So many times she'd pretended this was her house, instead of the boxy rambler with the patchy grass she shared with her parents and twin. And she was here so often—nearly every weekend or as often as her parents allowed before mandating some Johnson Family Time—sometimes it actually felt like her own home, like today.

She and Mari-Beth had gotten up, eaten egg-white omelets prepared by the Lintons' personal chef, took a nice long sit in the Jacuzzi and now were freshening their nails. She'd been outlining her thoughts to Mari-Beth about how she planned to deal with Mina at the Extreme. Sitting there on the cool, shiny hardwood floor in the room four times the size of Jessica's bedroom, gave her power. It surged through her like voltage, making her voice tremble with excitement.

That's what had gotten Mari-Beth's attention—the excitement in her voice.

It was typical that as soon as Jess slipped into the skin of Mari-Beth's luxe life and took on any role resembling the leader, Mari-Beth asserted her total BFF control, reminding Jess that she was only a visitor in the Lintons' paradise.

Jess could say no to polishing Mari-Beth's toes. MB didn't technically demand it. But Jess knew better.

She took the bottle and sat cross-legged in front of Mari-Beth. She brushed on a coat of polish, moved to the next foot and waited a few seconds for the polish to dry.

"I'm saying, what do you care who Mina hangs with? Not like she'll ever be down with us," Mari-Beth said. She shrugged like, *so what does it matter?*

Jess let a few seconds elapse, pretending to take great care to get the second coat of pink dazzle on smoothly. If she answered wrong, Mari-Beth, without saying it straight out of course, would trash Jess's whole plan and pull her support.

"Oh, I don't care who she hangs with," Jess said, rolling her eyes. "Where's the topcoat?"

Mari-Beth's professionally manicured fingernail pointed to her makeup table.

Jess pushed herself up and went searching in the nail polish tray, where forty bottles of polish sat in rainbow order, lightest to darkest. She plucked out the clear topcoat and sat back down.

This had to be Mari-Beth's idea if it was going to work. She had to phrase her answers just right.

And that's exactly where Jess and Mina were different—reason #110 Jess couldn't stand Mina in all her sunny optimism: The girl simply didn't live in the real world as far as Jess was concerned.

Mina wasn't cut out for popularity. It was too much work. And Jess had no problem letting Mina know that being middle of the pack was where she belonged. *I'm doing you a favor,* Jess thought, suppressing a chuckle.

Jess, on the other hand, knew how to play the game. Her friendship with MB was the perfect example. Even though the Lintons often had to foot the bill for Jess to come along, she was Mari-Beth's constant companion.

The price for admission to this world? Jess's total dedication to Mari-Beth. If Mari-Beth wanted it, Jess let her have it.

She followed Mari-Beth's lead and made sure the other Glams knew their place was well behind her. It was a full-time job playing second fiddle to Mari-Beth, especially when Jess wanted something that Mari-Beth didn't care about or was bored with.

Mari-Beth hugged her knees to her chest. Her toes dangled over the edge of the window seat for their final coat. Her voice had an annoyed edge to it when she said, "If you don't care, then why are we talking about her instead of calling Breck to see if he's definitely able to get the keg for Saturday's party?"

"I texted him a few minutes ago, remember?" Jess said, sure to keep the annoyance out of her own voice. "I'll ping him again when I finish your toes."

Mari-Beth's breath blew out in a warm stream over Jess's head as she sighed, "Okay, so what's this whole plan again?" She bit her lower lip, squinching her eyebrows. Her voice lost its edge. "I kind of like the part about the simul-text messages and pics." She erupted into a peel of giggles. "That part is cool."

Jess kept her head down and smiled as Mari-Beth offered suggestions on how to make the plan better.

"Let's just . . . forget we hate each other"

"Don't sweat girl, be yourself."
—Mary J. Blige, "Work That"

Mondays at Del Rio Bay High were either manic, the halls buzzing with the latest gossip from people high from their weekend antics, or eerily low-key, as if everyone was hung over from indulging in too much fun. With spring break only two days away, today was a manic Monday. Hall traffic moved faster, like getting to class sooner would help the day go faster, the students were rowdier and the teachers allowed louder shout-outs and unnecessary whoops without giving the "quiet" eye or a "shhh."

Mina whipped through the hall, a part of the Monday mania, anxious to get to lunch, easily her favorite subject lately. Her step stuttered when she heard her name called. She glanced back, but kept walking until it came again.

"Mi-naa."

Her insides froze as the familiar voice sang out again.

"Mi-naaa!"

It didn't matter that the voice sounded (friendly?) innocent enough.

"Mina, wait up."

It could have been any number of people calling out hello. But Mina knew the voice—that crisp proper tone, the way every letter of her name was sounded out, the unspoken command in it. In the seventh grade she'd heard it in her nightmares: "Mina, you're off the count! Mina, your low V's too low."

It had been the cheer year from hell and only one person held the honor of Head Cheer Devil—Jessica Johnson.

She willed her legs to slow down. People hustling to class brushed against her as she stemmed the natural flow of the traffic.

Her stomach churned. It wasn't fear. She simply hated dealing with Jessica. The drill was Jessica was snotty and Mina was indifferent, but always polite. But that was when Jessica saw Mina as a mid-pop, before Mina got the invite to the café. Now she and Jess were on equal footing.

Now that Mina rolled with the Upper cheer clique, she already had the one thing Jess had desperately sworn to keep out of Mina's grasp. She didn't have to play nice with Jess anymore.

Too bad her stomach hadn't gotten the memo. It grew increasingly woozy—from the usual weariness or something else, Mina couldn't tell.

She stopped in the middle of the hall and turned, slowly, toward the sound of Jess's voice, just in time to see Jessica take a few long, supermodel strides her way. Mina unconsciously scoured the hall for Mari-Beth Linton. But Jessica was alone.

Good. At least she'd only have to deal with one snot today.

"Are you heading to lunch?" Jessica asked. She stopped dead in front of Mina, legs slightly apart, hands on her hips in an end-of-the-runway pose and swished her thick weave. She was looking spring-cool in a pair of baby blue cotton capris, a matching blue baby doll tee with the words Queen Me across the chest, and sparkly American Eagle flops.

As Mina eyed Jess's gear on the sly, "Yeah," was her only response. It felt safe enough.

"No longer lounging in the middle of the pack, huh? Sara told me you're officially *in*, now." Jessica's hazel eyes glimmered and her mouth puckered—just a little—at the word "in" and for a second Mina caught what she thought was disgust. But it was gone before it ever registered, forcing Mina to chastise herself.

I've got to stop overanalyzing when it comes to Jess, she thought.

It took her a second to realize Jess had stopped talking and was waiting for a response.

"My bad. I didn't hear you. What did you say?" Mina asked, blinking herself back into the conversation.

Her face tight, Jessica visibly swallowed her annoyance. "I said," Jessica said with an exaggerated rise in her voice, "that I'll never figure out what my sister sees in you. Obviously she doesn't care that she and Kim may be responsible for the fall of the entire DRB social scene by inviting you in."

Ahhh, there was the Jessica Mina loved to hate. Her body actually relaxed as Jessica's insult reached her ears.

"Seriously, did you stop me to say that?" Mina asked, her voice its usual neutral when talking to Jess. Not loud enough to start an argument, but not low enough to signal defeat.

Jessica cocked her head, a smile on her lips, and snorted a haughty chuckle. "Actually, I did." She swished her hair again then nudged Mina's arm, signaling her to walk. People fanned out around them as they walked the center hall. "The Extreme is in a few days and we'll be stuck in O.C. together." She rolled her eyes and snorted, reminding Mina of a horse. "Look, I don't like you, Mina."

"Should I call a press conference?" Mina quipped, under her breath.

Jessica surprised her by laughing, a real, lusty laugh. Not the mechanical, Stepford-friends laugh that she and the other Glams had perfected. "Maybe you should, because I'm calling a truce."

Jessica stopped at the door to the cafeteria and turned to Mina. "You probably think now that you're in the café that you're an Upper and so we should get along, right?"

"Jess, believe it or not, I stopped trying to get along with you after the soc project," Mina said. She took a deep breath, steeling herself to say what she really felt instead of cowering from Jess's abrasive bluntness. "When we agreed it was cool that not everybody was going to be friends, I meant it. And that definitely applies to me and you. I'm swazy with that."

"Good, because that's real for us," Jessica said, her voice clipped. "Here's the thing. O.C. isn't that big. Even though I'm staying with Mari-Beth, we'll still end up partying in the same places during spring break . . ." She paused for dramatic effect, knowing no matter what status Mina thought she had, she wouldn't walk away before she was dismissed. Jess purposely took a second to wave to a few people before finishing. "I'm saying that from now through Sunday, let's just consider our differences squashed."

"Why?" Mina frowned.

"Because I don't feel like arguing with Sara about you the entire trip," Jessica said, matching the frown. "We don't need to be buds or anything. I'm just saying, until spring break ends, let's just . . . forget we hate each other."

Mina couldn't let it go. She pressed. "Wouldn't ignoring each other as usual be easier?"

"God, Mina, I'm waving the white flag! Is it a deal or what?"

The yelp caused a few people passing to turn and stare. But when they saw who it came from, they moved on.

Jessica waited, arms folded, her patience with Mina on empty.

Mina shifted uncomfortably from one foot to the other. She was the queen of positive, but this was Jessica Johnson. Mina had tried making peace with her the entire fall semester. And every time she did, Jess took the venom she spewed up a level.

Now a truce?

She needed time to soak it in, but the bell was about to ring and if Jessica's eyebrow arched any higher, it would meet her fake hairline.

"Yeah, we have a deal," Mina said finally.

"Great," Jessica said, thick with sarcasm. "Your indecisiveness *astounds* me," she huffed before supermodeling her way down the hall.

Mina stepped through the doors of the cafeteria and the heavy scent of grease à la mode made her already queasy stomach shrivel even more.

The snitty, clipped one-liners, cat-like glares, even Jess's keen sense for hitting below the belt—Mina thought she was used to it. Truce or not, her knees felt as if they were melting to her ankles.

She blew out a long breath and tried to let the normalcy of the cafeteria's rowdy banter bring her back from her clanging thoughts.

Her wobbly legs automatically carried her down the seven stairs and toward the door leading to the café. She joined the cheer table, where it was already standing room only, squeezing one slim shoulder between Jamie and Sara.

The five of them standing, front to back, looked as if they were playing a strange game of musical chairs, waiting in line ready to hop in the tall chairs the instant one of the three sitters got up. And the absurdity of it—standing so close at the teeny table with only one hand free to pick at her lunch—made Mina feel better.

There was plenty of space at the eight-seater tables inside the cafeteria. But she was here. After all Jessica's warnings that she'd never make it to the café as long as they both walked DRB High's halls, Mina could have been pinned between twenty people, standing on one leg—it would be swazy. But she was here.

"Hey, Mina, if you don't get that double-down cleaner, I think Coach Em is going to have an aneurysm," Kim said. She popped a low-fat chip into her mouth, grinning as she chewed.

The rest of the table laughed, no doubt at the image of Mina's flailing arms as she was tossed high enough to twist twice before landing safely in the hands of her bases. Mina's sloppy double-downs had been the reason for many of their suicide cycles of late.

Coach Embry was a taskmaster. Perfection, and nothing less, was her motto. Her tough tactics had made the team tight, quickly. They'd all been on the receiving end of her sharp tongue. Instead of feeling angry at Mina for not shaping up the stunt, they sympathized.

"What are you reaching for up there?" Jamie asked, nudging Mina playfully in the back of her knee.

"Anything," Mina quipped. Her heart did a tiny skip at the thought of the double twist. She hated them. "I'm trying, for real. But my arms . . ."

"Are going to knock somebody out, one day," Erica said, her brunette ponytail bobbing in confirmation.

Mina made sad eyes across the table at Kim and patted Sara's shoulder, joking with her bases. "Then I apologize in advance. But I swear I'll send flowers if you end up in the hospital."

Another round of laughter went up. With Nationals only days away the squad's nervous energy was at its peak. They were laughing now, but likely at practice, later, there would be tears and snapping one another's heads off for every missed step, stunt bobble and motion mistake.

Several Blue Devil basketball players, including Brian, and a few members of the lacrosse team joined the squad, forming a second circle of tight-knit standers.

"So what's the scoop, lady Blue Devils?" a curly-haired lacrosse player asked, managing to squeeze his way to the table. "You guys kicking booty at the Extreme or what?"

Mina joined the girls in a hearty "yeah," giggling as Brian stepped up close beside her. As the table talk went up a level, veering away from cheerleading and on to who would be hosting the expected beach party, Mina and Brian fell into their own zone.

Every day she expected to feel some sort of familiar comfort with Brian. But when they were together, her feet felt light and airy and her stomach did flip-flops, the good kind, not the kind she'd felt when Jessica called her in the hall.

She wished that feeling would never end.

Brian leaned in closer to her ear, each word tickling, sending her arms into goose bumps.

"This thing is going to be crazy," he said. "How y'all gonna find time to cheer in between all these parties I keep hearing about?"

Mina nodded. If the talk was to be believed, there were about four parties going down Friday night alone.

"Coach Em has us on curfew Friday night," she said, then shrugged. "She's letting us go to the Individuals. But trust, she *will* be herding us back to the hotel like cattle the second they're over."

Brian chuckled, low and deep.

The vibrations from his voice gave Mina's goose bumps, goose bumps.

He put his arms around her and rubbed her arms. "You cold?" he asked.

Mina laughed, embarrassed. The sun was shining right into the café's court, burning the chill in the air. But she wasn't about to explain. She ignored his question by starting a new conversation. "Are you excited about your first Extreme? It's mad crazy down there even when it's not spring break. But this year . . ." She shook her head as if that completed her thought.

"Oh I'm curious about it, for sure. People are hyped," Brian said. He nuzzled her. "But I'm more pressed about being with you the whole weekend."

"Well, me and my parents," Mina reminded him.

His thick black curls blew as a slight breeze zipped through the café. He whipped a perfectly creased cap from his back pocket and sat it lightly atop his head as he teased, "What else is new?"

Mina elbowed his stomach. But she was lucky. Brian was a good sport about having to hang out at her house under her parents' cool eye whenever they weren't with the entire clique. They rarely had real alone time. Scratch that, they *never* had any alone time. Papa and Mama Bear Mooney made sure of it.

The Extreme would be different. She'd already warned her parents that the cheer squad had lots of bonding plans. As long as she was with the girls . . . well, near the girls, her parents wouldn't question it. She and Brian were going to get some time to themselves if she had anything to do with it.

As if reading her mind, he said, "But your moms and pops not planning to crash the beach with us, are they?"

Mina rolled her eyes at the thought. She could seriously see her parents trying. But they were old pros at cheer events. Mina knew they'd gladly find other things to do rather than have their ears pierced by the girls' constant, rowdy giggling and multi-group conversations.

"Nope," Mina answered, a smile in her voice and on her face. "You'll have me all to yourself on beach night."

Doubts

Later that afternoon, Mina turned around in the passenger seat to look Michael in the eye. Only half-teasing, she asked, "So remind me again why you're ditching on my first Nationals as a Blue Devil?"

His dark chocolate face pleaded with her to drop this, not to have this conversation with Brian in the car. Mina got the message loud and clear, but wasn't having it. Torn between understanding that Mike had his own thing, and totally irked that he'd choose Nationals weekend to do it, had her feeling especially pouty. She pressed when there was no immediate answer. "Seriously, Mike, you know I need all you guys there giving me that good juju."

"I'm breaking the karmic chain?" Michael grinned.

"Why yes, in fact you are," Mina said primly, but she couldn't keep a straight face. She turned sideways in the seat, tucking her legs beneath her so she could see into the back of Brian's Explorer, where Michael sat directly behind her. Her voice lost its pouty bossiness as she pleaded, "You know I would never ask you to choose between your fashion gig and me . . ."

"Except you are," Brian said. He took one hand off the wheel for a hot second, so Michael could lean forward and give him a pound. His large eyes narrowed as he gazed Mina's way, smiling slyly.

She gave his arm a light shove then turned down the Go-Go music, which Brian kept on constant blast.

"No, I'm not." She squinted in concentration, turning back to Michael. "For real, Mike, I'm not asking you to choose. But . . . I mean, I just really want you there."

"Diva, you know Brian and JZ gon' hold it down for you," Michael said. "And you can call me fifty-eleven times a day to update me if you want. I swear I won't screen your calls."

He and Brian laughed good at that one.

Mina turned front again, letting it go. She wasn't going to win this one.

"The turn right here, son?" Brian asked, looking in his rearview at Michael's nodding head.

"Yeah, just on your left where that big marquee is." Michael pointed. "I appreciate you dropping me off, kid."

"No problem." Brian glanced over at the silent Mina. He poked her side, pushed her knee and plucked at her to tease her out of her mood. "Man, you know the drama I would have caught if I'd said no."

"You could have said no. It wouldn't have mattered to me," Mina huffed. Hearing the bratty tone of her own voice, she peeked back over the seat, in time to see a flash of hurt on Michael's face. She smiled sheepishly. "Alright, so I'm acting like Jessica, right?" she said, referencing Jess instead of using the word "bitch." To her they were often one and the same. She got the chuckle she wanted from Michael. "My bad." She tapped his knee lightly with her fist. "I just wanted you there. But I know it's a big deal that you're gonna be working on costumes for The Players."

"Well, I let you slide this time with that 'tude. I don't want to embarrass you in front of Brian," Michael said.

But it wasn't his usual acid-tongued response. They'd been friends long enough to read one another's thoughts. Mina suspected Michael felt more and more like the fifth wheel now that she and Brian were together so often. If it weren't the whole clique hanging out, and even sometimes when it was, Michael made himself busy with Bay Dra-Da or spending time with Rob, a dancer with The Players.

She hadn't meant to make Michael feel bad about not going. She made up for it with gossip. "Ooh, speaking of Jessica, you won't believe this," Mina said. She regaled Michael and Brian with the story of Jessica temporarily squashing their beef, sharing both her skepticism and weary relief.

"I wouldn't trust that." Michael shook his head. "You know how she is."

"I think y'all being hard on ol' girl," Brian said. "She seems alright to me."

"Pssh." Mina rolled her eyes. "Okay, new boy. You have no idea." She struggled to put her pool of thoughts on Jess into a simple sentence, but only came back with, "Jessica wouldn't know friendly if it smacked her in the face."

"Alright, yeah she's definitely a diva. And I can see she's mad bossy. But . . ." Brian shrugged. "Twins are tight. So I can see her doing this for her sister. You sound a little paranoid." He snickered. "You act like she out to get you."

"She is," Mina said. She looked to Michael, her eyes prompting him to agree. A twinge of disappointment pinched her when Michael's face remained neutral and he shrugged. She slid slowly back into her seat, facing front once more.

She'd wanted, needed really, Michael to set her mind at ease. If not agree with her, maybe give some advice on how to steer through this truce without getting burned. But his silence spoke volumes. She'd hurt his feelings by snapping on him in front of Brian. They could do that when it was just the two of them—or if it was a true joking diss session with everyone around—but Mina had been genuinely snotty about it.

It wasn't cool and she knew it.

"Well, I don't know about out to get me, but there's always been bad blood between us," she muttered finally.

Michael's continued silence spoke louder than Brian's, "You're paranoid, toughie. Just chill and ride with it." But Mina tried to take stock in his words, just the same. What else could she do?

See what my girls think, she suddenly thought to herself, the idea giving her needed comfort.

Later, she chatted online with Jacinta, Lizzie and Kelly and IM'd with Carla about Spanish homework. Although the worksheet with fifty vocabulary words was getting left in the dust amid the cyber convos, it was getting done . . . sort of.

How in the world did people multitask before the invention of Instant Messaging, Mina wondered.

She couldn't imagine trying to do this back in the day, when dialing someone up on the telephone was the only way to go. First of all, her mother would come running the second she heard Mina's chattering. Second, unless you wore an earpiece with a mic, holding the phone between the shoulder and chin was so 1990s.

She laughed aloud as Carla asked for the answer to number thirty—the same word Mina was having a problem with. Instinctively she looked it up on a free translation site, and keyed in the answer. She cracked up at Carla's response.

Imacutie: did u get that frm spanish4dumes?
BubbliMi: YUP
Imacutie: I went to another site and got a totally different answer

"Shoot," Mina exclaimed. The sites were horribly unreliable. When she'd first discovered them she'd sworn she'd sail through Spanish with ease. Then Ms. Cortez, her Spanish teacher, had chosen Mina's paper as an example of how not to translate. And that had been the end of that . . . well, that had been the end of using it regularly. She still used it for simple vocab words. And the sites were still, obviously, the worst solution ever for foreign language slackers like her and Carla.

She responded to Carla and saw that the chat with the clique was getting interesting. The truth was, they could have been debating the merits of paint drying and it would have been more exciting than her homework. She tapped off a quick "l8r" to Carla, barely giving her a chance to get in her own goodbye, before pushing the homework aside and placing herself comfortably in the middle of the ongoing chat.

She muted the loud ringing of each IM to preempt any parental intervention.

Liz-e-O: so r u guys down 4 hooking up over break? Pls say yes. I cannot sit home w/the 'rents for 3 days!
CinnyBon: mos def' I don't see whas the big deal about the Xtreme anyway
K-Lo: I'm in

Mina jumped right in defending the event.

BubbliMi: don't get it twisted the Xtreme is THE biggest cheer event in MD but I think the hype is cuz its during spring break. Been years since that happened.
CinnyBon: where u been Princess?!
BubbliMi: Spanish HW. Sry I had 2 keep dippin out
Liz-e-O: hello this is about the Losers NOT going to Freak Fest err . . . I mean the Xtreme LOL
BubbliMi: not 2 rub it in . . . but I think it's definitely gonna be some wildin' out
CinnyBon: Lizzie u gon' stop all that loser talk or we gon' throw some bows up in here.

Liz-e-O: ;-)

K-Lo: we could get 2gether at my place. Grand wouldn't mind

CinnyBon: hanging out at the mansion again? So boring. j/k

Mina snickered. They never tired of chilling at Kelly's big house with the theater room, tennis courts, swimming pool and music studio. With so much to do, right there, it was the ideal sleepover spot and not just because Kelly lived in the most exclusive nabe in Del Rio Bay. Kelly's grandmother welcomed them with open arms. She was so excited that Kelly had such a nice group of friends, Mina suspected the girls could stay over every weekend and Mrs. Lopez would be swazy with it.

Every now and then they'd walk to the country club for "teen" night or the park located in the center of the neighborhood and bump into Jessica and Mari-Beth, who lived one street down from Kelly. There were always a few tense, awkward minutes as the girls teetered on the edge of indecision—say hello or ignore one another—before Mari-Beth said something snide and uncalled for, breaking the ice and keeping the world from spinning off its axis, which she seemed to think would happen if she wasn't a snot.

Which reminded Mina. She brought the girls up to speed on her latest encounter with Jessica. Her friends wasted no time giving their .02.

CinnyBon: eeent I wouldn't trust that!

Liz-e-O: Ok whas "eent"?

BubbliMi: 4 real

CinnyBon: like a buzzer, u know wrong answer. Mina leave that madness alone. Go on ignoring Jess and b about ur business. 4 real

K-Lo: Mayb she's sincere Cin. I believe Jess would do it for Sara. They're twins and close.

Mina expected that from Kelly. She was the only person Mina knew, other than herself, who attempted to make lemonade out of any lemons thrown at her.

Liz-e-O: well as close as anyone can b 2 Jess w/o getting burnt to a crisp by her heat-seeking cruelty

BubbliMi: ROFL I know thas right!

CinnyBon: w/e. y'all 2 new 4 me . . . always so . . . hopeful

Liz-e-O: umm . . . and that's bad cuz?

BubbliMi: let's not even get started. I know how Jess is but I'll take her 4 her word. Moving on! Cinny I thought u were go-n home this weekend?

CinnyBon: not if I can help it

K-Lo: Y? sounds like u and Raheem been getting along better

Liz-e-O: says who?

CinnyBon: Somebody done told u wrong!

BubbliMi: Kell holding back on us. U got scoop which means u been talking 2 Angel. Y'all back on again?

K-Lo: sort of

CinnyBon: that must mean yes and instead of handling y'all own biz u talking about mine

BubbliMi: r u 2 back Cinny? Nothing wrong w/that?

Mina guessed. Even though Kelly and Angel's *should we date/shouldn't we date* had gone on longer than their actual thirty–day relationship, and Jacinta was up and down about Raheem more than an elevator, she was determined to be supportive of her friends' BF decisions. They were of hers.

CinnyBon: we're not back 2gether

K-Lo: u mean officially?

CinnyBon: K jus say what u know cuz these questions r on my last nerve!

Liz-e-O: u've been called 2 the mat K-Lo

BubbliMi: dish! Dish!

K-Lo: LOL Angel said when ur home u hang out w/them and that sometimes u and Raheem ::ahem:: hang out alone

Liz-e-O: ::smooches::

CinnyBon: n that = us being back 2gether how?

Liz-e-O: umm . . . cuz ur not just hooking up w/any ol' body right?

CinnyBon: no but . . . look it's a long story. We not back 2gether. Real talk!

Mina jumped in and changed the subject. She could practically see Jacinta's face—eyebrows mashed together in a V, lips pursed and neck rolling as she typed.

BubbliMi: Kel, when were u gonna tell us about u and Angel?

CinnyBon: yeah little Miss Can't-Handle-The-Hustle

K-Lo: I was going 2 tell u guys. It just happened Saturday. But Angel's giving up hustling so we're gonna start from scratch

BubbliMi: WHAT?!

CinnyBon: yeah right.

Liz-e-O: is he serious abt it?

K-Lo: well I think he's serious

CinnyBon: no harm Kell but u know a playa will say anything 2 get w/u

BubbliMi: if he's serious thas cool K!

Liz-e-O: mayb u'll be the 1st to turn a bad boy good

CinnyBon: y'all blve him?! Again—Y'all 2 new 4 me LOL

BubbliMi: Cinny come on he doin it 4 luv <3 <3 Yay luv

K-Lo: LOL

Liz-e-O: Yay luv?! see even I'm not that new, Cinny.

CinnyBon: I'll belve it when I see it thas all I'm sayin

K-Lo: guess we should say the same 'bout u and Raheem being over

Liz-E-O: Ouch Cinny she told u

BubbliMi: Kelly—1 Cinny—1 Match point

CinnyBon: w/e boogee princesses we hung out 2 or 3 times no big deal. We still friends. That's all!

BubbliMi: friends w/benes

Liz-e-O: Like u and JZ b/coming friends? ::smooches::

CinnyBon: now there u go. U worse than Mina. I jus like flirting w/JZ and his fine azz

BubbliMi: um-hmmm . . .

CinnyBon: y'all r seriously up in my biz. w/friends like u I don't need enemies fo' sho'

BubbliMi: its cuz we luv u. Yay luv! LOL

Liz-e-O: ok don't u have Spanish hw 2 do? j/k

BubbliMi: actually I do. L8r dudettes

Reluctantly, Mina exited the chat and let the Spanish vocabulary words roll off her tongue in hopes that saying them aloud would help her understand their meaning.

"Just yes or no . . . do you wanna go?"

"Forget yesterday, we'll make the great escape."
—Boys Like Girls, "The Great Escape"

The chat marched on without Mina for another half hour, talk bouncing between a possible sleepover at Kelly's and Kelly and Angel's second attempt at the boyfriend/girlfriend thing, before ending in a loose plan, but strong vow, to make this the "least-suckiest-spring-break-ever-even-though-we're-the-only-ones-not-going-to-the-Extreme."

After signing off Jacinta fumed.

She was going to get Angel. Him and his big mouth, telling Kelly about her and Raheem.

It wasn't that she was hiding her weekends with Raheem from the girls . . . okay, she was. But in her defense, she'd been struggling from day one to keep her two worlds from colliding. Being in The Cove wasn't like being in The Woods. She felt right at home in both neighborhoods. But sometimes clicking over from one mind-set to another was unsettling, like traveling from the earth to the moon's zero gravity.

After all the advice she gave her friends about life, love and the pursuit of a decent boyfriend, she'd look like a hypocrite, not to mention weak, to go back with Raheem after he'd shamed her by kissing another girl the night of the party while she was only a few feet away.

That's exactly why she wasn't going home over spring break. She'd decided for sure as soon as her father's Navigator crossed the DRB Bridge Sunday morning.

Fridays and Saturdays were hard enough. She wasn't about to spend four days at home, tempted to race out of the house each time Angel called. She knew exactly where she wanted to be during break—O.C. And not because of the cheer competition either.

The idea had come to her on Sunday afternoon when Mina hyped over JZ's flirting. Jacinta laughed aloud at the thought of Mina's nagging. Sometimes she and JZ flirted just to set her off. Jacinta was surprised Mina hadn't figured that out yet.

It was all in fun.

JZ wasn't interested in doing the exclusive thing with anyone. And Jacinta wasn't looking for a new boyfriend. They made the perfect flirt match. She liked hanging out with him because, ironically, he reminded her a little of Raheem, only without the drama.

The more Jacinta thought about trekking down to O.C. with the guys, the more it made sense.

It would be the perfect distraction. A whole weekend away, no Raheem, no slipping back. It's just what she needed to prove, once and for all, that she and Raheem were really over.

All she had to do was convince Lizzie and Kelly to roll with her. Kelly would be easy. Since going out with Angel, Kelly was down for more than people might assume from someone so quiet.

Lizzie's going to be the tough one, Jacinta thought. She hopped into bed knowing exactly how to get Lizzie on board.

The next afternoon, she texted Lizzie and waited by the auditorium until she emerged. As she expected, Lizzie balked at the idea.

"Come on, Lizzie," Jacinta said, her voice coming as close to pleading as it ever got. "Do you really feel like sitting home doing nothing the whole break?" Her eyes flashed skepticism in her honey brown face.

"I thought we were just going to hang at Kelly's," Lizzie said. She scanned the empty hall nervously, as if expecting someone to pop their scheming right then and there.

Cinny immediately pounced, anticipating Lizzie's reluctance. "Well, change of plans." She pulled Lizzie into the dark auditorium, where only minutes before Lizzie had been helping to pack away props and costumes.

They sat in the last row of the huge auditorium, cloaked in darkness. The busy stage was the only brightly lit area. Trunks were opened, closed and pushed across the stage as the heavy period-piece costumes were stored. No one from the stage even looked their way.

"What are you still doing here, anyway?" Lizzie whispered.

"Track," Jacinta said. "We ended early." She rubbed absently at her sore thighs, savoring the pain even as she winced. Before Lizzie could say another word, Jacinta blurted, "If you want to go to the Extreme, I know how we can roll." She lowered her voice more as it echoed softly back. "Before you make up excuses . . . just yes or no, do you wanna go?"

"Yeah, I do," Lizzie said. She looked toward the stage to see if anyone noticed them. But Ms. Jessamay was shouting directions amid the general chatter.

"Alright, my aunt is going to New York for her job," Jacinta said. She leaned in closer to Lizzie and Lizzie leaned in, too. Their foreheads nearly touched, making them a strange mixed-race Siamese twin—one a natural blonde, the other blonde thanks to the magic of hair dye. "I begged her to let me stay home instead of going to my father's house. And she finally said yes."

Lizzie's eyes widened. "How'd you do that?"

Jacinta chuckled and waved it off. "I told her that I didn't want to go home and have to be so close to Raheem for four days." Her eyebrows jumped as she shrugged. "Which is sort of true. If I went home, it would be impossible not to run into him." She exhaled softly. "I'm not down for that this weekend."

Lizzie clucked in sympathy.

"Anyway, so she said it was cool as long as I checked in with my father every night," Jacinta continued.

"Wait . . . how are you going to do that from O.C.?" Lizzie fretted.

"Look, I'll just call him every night from my cell. I have the feature where I can get my number forwarded to Aunt Jacqi's home number. When I call it will look like I'm calling from there."

Lizzie groaned softly. "I don't know, Cinny."

Jacinta grabbed Lizzie's wrist and shook it firmly. "It can work, Lizzie. Your parents will let you stay over, won't they?"

Lizzie's mouth twisted as she considered the question.

"They don't even need to know Aunt Jacqi won't be home," Jacinta said, correctly reading the worry on Lizzie's face. "Look, our parents are so used to us all doing S.O.'s they barely even check anymore with each other."

Lizzie nodded slowly, still unsure. "I guess . . . but what if they do?" she asked.

Jacinta sat back in her seat, thought about it then shrugged. "They won't."

"Cinny, my mom will know something is wrong as soon as I ask," Lizzie said. Her brows knitted in worry. "I can't . . ."

"You're an actress. Just act," Jacinta reasoned.

"I'm not that good," Lizzie mumbled.

"Okay. I'll call and ask your mother for you. How 'bout that?" Jacinta looked in Lizzie's eyes. "Just let me handle it. Okay?"

Lizzie gnawed at her thumbnail.

Jacinta's smile gleamed through the dimness as she said, "You know you wanna hang out with your boy, T." She whispered loudly, "You in?"

Lizzie hunched her shoulders to her ears then let them go with a huge sigh as she nodded.

Jacinta grinned. "For real, I'll take care of everything."

Live a Little

"What you know 'bout me? What you know?"
—Lil' Mama, "Lip Gloss"

Hours later, Jacinta made good on her word.

With her advice, "You're an actress. Just act," chiming in Lizzie's ears, she blanked her mind of the road trip and hanging with Todd and focused instead on tomorrow's Algebra II exam.

Nothing like a good algebraic equation to numb your brain, she thought, letting the familiarity of the numbers lull her to the homework zone.

She jumped when the phone rang beside her, breaking her concentration.

Frowning at the number shining back at her on the screen, it took a full two seconds to recognize it was Jacinta calling. In the four months they'd been friends, Jacinta had never called her house before. And even though Lizzie had known Cinny was going to call tonight, hearing Jacinta's "Hey, girl" on the other end was still odd. They IM'd all the time, but never talked on the phone.

"Hey," Lizzie said, dumbstruck, as if the call were coming from another planet.

"You cool, right?"

Lizzie caught herself nodding, then whispered, "Yeah."

"Okay. Let me talk to your moms real quick."

Heading for her bedroom door, Lizzie froze when Jacinta's voice hollered, "Hey, Lizzie!"

"What?" Lizzie whispered.

Jacinta laughed. "Why are you whispering?"

Lizzie chuckled. "I did tell you how bad I am about schemes, right?"

"I see. No, I was just going to say, remember to act surprised that I'm asking you to my house."

"Don't think that's gonna be a problem," Lizzie muttered. "Okay, I'm heading downstairs. Hold on."

Her voice was still tinged with surprise when she walked into the family room and handed over the phone. "Mom. Cinny wants to ask you something."

"Cinny?" Her mom's eyebrows caterpillared together in confusion. She took the phone. "Hi Jacinta. It's Mrs. O'Reilly."

Lizzie sat beside her on the couch and continued playing dumb, gazing at her mom throughout the one-sided conversation.

Lying she was bad at. Acting, she could handle.

Blank. Blank. Keep your mind blank, she chanted to herself.

"A sleepover huh?" her mom said into the phone. She trained her deep green eyes on Lizzie when she said, "I swear, you girls never get enough of each other."

Lizzie smiled and shrugged. Her mom ran her hands through Lizzie's hair. "Well Cinny, you're proof that Lizzie isn't the *only* person in the world not going to the Extreme."

Lizzie's cheeks flashed pink.

"Should we drop her over to your house on Friday?" her mom said, making Lizzie's heart stop for a second. It galloped on when her mom said, "Oh, I guess that's fine. He's going to drop you guys straight to your house, right?"

They talked on for a few more seconds before her mom said, "Okay. I'm sure you girls will have a good time. Do you want to talk to Lizzie? Hmm . . . oh, okay. Bye, sweetie." She hung up. "Cinny's going to call you back in about ten minutes."

With a mix of skepticism and hope in her voice Lizzie asked, "So I can stay?"

"Yes. I'm glad you have some plans for the weekend." Her mom folded her arms. "See, now this won't be the worstspringbreakever, Miss Drama Queen, USA."

"Maybe not the worst," Lizzie agreed.

Her mom laughed. "Well, how does Mina feel about you guys sleeping over without her? Does that break one of her friendship rules?"

"This has all met her approval," Lizzie assured her. "She even gave us some suggestions. We'll probably go see the new Nick Cannon movie."

"Well don't run Miss Jacqi to death, Friday night," her mom warned.

"We won't." The phone rang and Lizzie picked up before the second ring. She went to her room, taking two steps at a time as Jacinta gave her an update.

"Okay, I still need to call and ask Mrs. Lopez," Jacinta said. "But I think she'll let Kelly go."

"To O.C.?" Lizzie scowled.

Jacinta sucked her teeth. "To my house, Liz." She emphasized every word, hammering the story into Lizzie's head. "Remember, we're having a sleepover . . . right? A sleepover at my crib."

Lizzie nodded along, trying to keep the truth separate from the lie.

"Sleepover, sleepover, sleepover," she chanted under her breath. She took a seat on the carpet in her room. "Next time, you guys just kidnap me so I won't know the truth about where we're going. Makes it easier for me to play dumb."

"I'll keep that in mind," Jacinta laughed.

Lizzie hugged her knees to her chest. "I can't believe I'm doing this."

"Live a little, girl," Jacinta teased.

Lizzie rolled her eyes. "If we're caught, I won't be living at all."

"We won't get caught," Jacinta assured her.

To Lizzie's surprise, Jacinta's confidence was infectious. She made the whole plan seem so innocent and logical. "And we're gonna surprise Mina, okay?" Jacinta said. "So don't tell her you're rolling down there."

A happy chill tap-danced down Lizzie's spine. This was just the type of action Mina would love a piece of. She couldn't wait to see Mina's face when they burst into the arena Friday night.

"Oh my God, she's going to freak."

"I know. Until then just chill," Jacinta instructed. "Just plan it like a regular sleepover. Right?"

"Right," Lizzie said. She twirled a strand of hair around her fingers and let it unfurl on its own as she declared, "Man, the things we do for love."

Jacinta chuckled wryly. "Puh . . . trust, I've done dumber things for it."

Lizzie didn't argue. But in her mind she thought, *dumber than sneaking away for the weekend without anyone knowing?*

Doubtful.

A Kink in the Plan

"I feel like slapping somebody today (slap, slap)."
—Ludacris, "Slap"

Heat rose in Jessica's cheeks. Swallowing hard, she tried to suppress the storm welling in her chest. Maybe she'd heard her father wrong. Her fork clattered to her plate, dinner forgotten, and she pierced her father with narrowed eyes as if it might help her comprehend better.

Her father sipped from his glass, smiled and completed his announcement about the family riding down to O.C. together. "So we're all set. Your grandparents can't wait to see us tomorrow."

"But you said I could ride down with the Lintons," Jess said. The calm in her voice belied the emotional maelstrom roiling in her chest. Only her face, set in classic Jess argument mode, hinted at the tantrum to come.

She gazed across the table at Sara, their twin senses silently communicating.

Sara blanched. She looked as if she wanted to duck. Instead, she sat back in her seat and moved the mashed potatoes, gravy and pork chop around on her plate as Jess demanded, "Why? Why can't I ride down with the Lintons? You said I could."

She folded her arms as if to say, "this better be good."

Their dad, always the picture of calm in the face of her storms, smiled. His brown eyes and coffee-bean complexion were the same as Jessica's. So were his long, lean body and strong will. He was the one match Jessica had never conquered. "Because it's been awhile since we've traveled as a family," he said calmly. "I want to spend some time with my girls before you all disappear into the crowd at the beach."

"Your dad and I miss Johnson Family Time," their mom said. She stood beside her husband's chair, beaming. A petite blonde, whose face was Sara's without the rich, light-cocoa coloring, Jennifer Johnson looked from one of her twins to the other and her eyes began to tear. "You girls are always either gone with friends, at some activity or another, or squirreled away upstairs on that computer. It's been harder and harder to force some time into the schedule for us to bond without one of your friends underfoot. Can't Dad and I have two hours with just the four of us?"

Jessica scowled. She pulled her arms tighter against her chest. "But Mom, you guys promised I could ride with the Lintons weeks ago."

"How about this? You can ride back with them," their dad said. He scooped a mouthful of mashed potatoes into his mouth.

"Jess, look, we gave up last year's vacation because, luckily, Daddy and the band were booked solid." Proud, Jennifer gave her husband's shoulder a squeeze. "This will sort of be like a make-up trip."

"Why not the ride back, then?" Jess begged. "If you're going to let me ride with the Lintons I choose the ride down."

"No. We already promised your grandparents we'd stop and see them on the way down," their dad said. He stood up and kissed his wife on the cheek. "Dinner was good, baby. I'm going downstairs to rehearse."

With that he disappeared down the hall. The sounds of his footsteps on the stairs dimmed and then a door shut, signaling Jessica to begin the real assault.

"I don't get it. Everything was set and now just out of the blue you want Johnson Family Vacation?" she snapped. Her lip pooched in a childish pout.

Unfazed, her mom cleared the table. But without her husband to help weather the storm, her voice was weary. "Jessica, why must *everything* be a battle, honey? Is family time that unappetizing to you?"

Jessica carried her plate to the sink, simmering down the venom in her voice. She could feel her mom wanting to give in. "Mom, family time is cool. But Mari-Beth and I have already made plans." She stood her ground near the sink, pleading quietly with her mom. "Please, just let me ride down with them and then ride back home with you guys."

"Grand and Pop are already expecting us . . . but . . ." her mother said, wavering.

"We can stop on the way back. They won't mind," Jessica pressed. Her voice took on the happy lilt of someone about to get their way.

Strains of smooth jazz floated through the house. For a second, the two Johnson women were silent as they listened to the saxophone's call.

Sara joined her sister and mom near the sink, making their pair a triangle. She handed her plate over and was about to walk off when her mom said, not unkindly, "No, Jess. Daddy's planned a fun trip down to O.C. Honestly, why can't you be more easygoing like Sara?" She rubbed Jess's arm. "It'll be fun. I promise."

"How can it be fun when I'm practically being held hostage?" Jess sneered. "I can't believe you guys are breaking a promise."

Sara, always the compromiser, interjected. "Hey, Mom, I bet Grandma and Pop would love for us to stop by on Sunday, instead. Then we could have a big dinner with them."

Jessica's face lit up. Yes! Sunday dinner. *Good one, Sara,* she thought, sending her twin telepathic kudos.

Their mom shook her head. "Sorry, girls. It's a good idea. But

Dad wants to stop on the way down." As she waited for the water to fill the sink, she pulled her hair back into a ponytail.

Jessica turned heel and stalked out of the room. She lingered around the corner, listening as Sara whisper-shouted, "Mom."

"What, sweetie?" her mom asked.

"Please stop telling Jess to be more like me. She hates when you do that . . ." Sara sighed. "And so do I."

"Oh you know your sister. If she wasn't dramatic I'd think something was wrong," their mother said, then began humming along to the saxophone riff floating through the house.

If they expected her to be dramatic, Jess certainly wasn't about to disappoint. She stomped down the hallway and slammed her bedroom door. Seconds later, Sara knocked.

Jess knew it was Sara, because there was a pause: Knock-knock, then nothing.

Sara was the only one in the family who honored Jess's policy of knocking and waiting for an invite.

At least someone respects my wishes around here, Jess thought bitterly.

She blew out a big breath of exasperation before finally calling out "come in" to her twin. She stayed in front of her mirror, brushing her hair vigorously as if it were on fire.

Sara burst in and flopped on the bed. She propped herself on one shoulder, watching Jess in the mirror.

Minutes passed with no words between the twins.

This was part of their routine when Jess didn't get her way. Jess the vent-er, Sara the listener.

As Sara waited quietly, Jess took her time, like she always did, a silent unceremonious countdown to an outburst.

Three . . . Jess grabbed a water bottle from the stand beside her and gave it several hearty pumps.

Two . . . Jess's fingers ran through her hair until it was saturated. The auburn weave began to crinkle. In a matter of seconds, it was just as curly as Sara's.

One . . . Jess fluffed the hair, satisfied it was curly enough, then pulled the top half into a ponytail. She took a few more lackluster squirts with the water before slamming the bottle down and declaring, "Mom and Dad are impossible." She faced Sara, leaning against the wall, her arms folded. The words poured out, an angry stream of frustration. "Just because we finally have lives of our own, they're getting all sentimental and sappy, treating us like we're still in elementary school." Her voice was an exaggerated, dopey whine. "Family time. We need more family time."

She rolled her eyes and ranted on. "Mari-Beth is going to have a frickin' cow when I tell her. And she'll probably ask Simone to go with her instead." She slammed her fists into her thighs and let out a random scream. "I've gotta find a way to change their minds."

Sara waited a second—she always did. A strategy, Jessica was sure, so it wouldn't seem like she wasn't listening.

"It sucks. But you know it won't be all bad." Sara teased, "Grand might make some of her strawberry cupcakes."

Jessica rolled her eyes. Her arms went back to their tight lock against her chest. "Gross, Sara. I haven't eaten those things in years."

"You ate them at Christmastime," Sara bit back, annoyed.

"Whatever. They have like a bazillion calories in them." Jessica turned back to the mirror and fiddled with her hair.

"I'm on your side, Jess. Don't be a snot," Sara scolded.

Jessica caught a glimpse of Sara's pinched face in the mirror. It didn't take twin sense to know Sara had reached her limit. She toned down her acidic tongue.

"I swore off Grand's strawberry cupcakes as my New Year's resolution." She walked over and sat on the foot of the bed. "You should too or you won't fit in that teeny tiny cheer uniform."

She poked at Sara's muscular—but nowhere near fat—thigh and they laughed.

Jess rarely admitted it (had never actually spoken the words aloud) but she knew Sara had her back. And even though Jess gave

Sara plenty of 'tude, mostly venting about someone else who was on her nerves, she loved their twin connection—needed it, in fact.

Their parents were constantly trying to get Jess to ease up, calm down, and otherwise be more Johnson-like.

Mari-Beth demanded everything her way. Their friendship was exhausting.

Sara was the only person who took Jess for herself, warts and all.

Jess groaned. Her usual defensive, clipped tone slipped into sisterly complaining. It was a side only Sara ever saw and even she saw it rarely.

"This sucks, Sara."

"That you can't go with Mari-Beth or that you have to tell her you can't go?" Sara asked, eyebrow cocked high.

"Both," Jess admitted. "And Simone's bucking for my spot. I just know it. The little witch."

Sara shook her head. "And *these* are your best friends. You can definitely have that."

Jess shrugged. "Nobody said friendship was easy."

"Nobody said it had to be that much work, either." Sara sat up and crossed her legs. "Hey, speaking of work. What's this I hear about you and Mina trucing?"

Jessica's eyebrows raised. "What, did Mina go yell it over the loudspeaker?"

"No. She told me at practice today. Said you and her are waving the white flag until after the Extreme." Sara narrowed her eyes. "What's that all about? I thought your hate for Mina was what kept you alive?"

Jessica laughed. "Dramatic much, Sara?" She pushed herself back on the bed until her back was against the wall. "Well, don't get it twisted. We're not friends. But if she's going to be underfoot the entire spring break . . ." Jessica cut her eyes over to Sara. "Thanks in large part to you. I'm just saying, I know how weird you felt when the soc project sleepover was over here and she and I kept fighting."

Jess shrugged. It was always painful for her to show any weakness or vulnerability. Her voice was a mix of tough and gentle as she said, "I'm trying to help *you* out."

"Help *me* out huh?"

"Yes, help *you* out." Jessica shoved Sara's legs with her foot.

"Really?" Sara asked, genuinely surprised.

"It's not a big deal, Sara," Jessica said, clipped voice back in action. "I may not even survive three straight days of Mina. Especially now that I'm not staying with MB until Thursday. One more day for her to drive me nuts. But you like her." Her eyes rolled in a clear, "God knows why?" motion. "And no doubt you guys will be hanging out the entire time. So . . ." Jess swished her hair then exhaled with the effort. "I'll suck it up for a few days. But once the Extreme is over . . ." She shrugged as if to say, who knows. "Oh, but do me a favor, please."

Sara raised her eyebrows in question.

"We're making a massive cellie list so we can text people about where the parties are and stuff. Can you get the numbers of Mina, Brian and the rest of her . . ." She snorted lightly before spitting out the word, "Clique." Her smile was sly but her eyes playful. "I mean, if they're interested in being down with the hottest parties."

"Oh you know she's down. I'll get the numbers," Sara said.

Jess gave her sister a fleeting smile of appreciation before pushing herself off the bed. She walked over to the closet, abruptly closing the discussion.

At least some parts of the plan were still falling into place.

Truce'n

"One night only, let's not pretend to care."
—Dreamgirls, "One Night Only"

Welcome Cheerleaders!

Two . . . three . . . four . . .

Mina counted each store sign and hotel marquee that eagerly predicted the onslaught of spirit chicks. Their arrival was the appetizer before the feast. Summer season started in forty-five days. When it did, the hotels, beach and every other nook and cranny of the tiny ten-mile island, Assawoman Bay on one side, the Atlantic on the other, would be packed daily through Labor Day.

She was up to seven welcome signs after only three minutes on the four-lane highway that ran the length of O.C. And those were only the businesses on the beach side. The road, scrunched between high-rise hotels, suspect-looking motels and enough T-shirt shops to outfit the entire state of Maryland with "I'm Crabby in O.C. MD" tees, stretched in front of her father's Navigator.

She was here. Let the Upper revelry begin.

She opened her phone and tapped off a message to Sara:

here! Watchu doin

Then to Lizzie:

here! How wuz da test

Then Michael:

baby boy wat up?!

Finally to Brian:

miss ya already

Mina danced, wiggling in her seat to the music from the truck's radio as she waited for signs of life from home.

The music went to a whisper as her mom said, "Our room probably isn't ready. So how about we hit the shops?"

"Sounds good," Mina said, one eye on the phone. "I wouldn't be mad if we ate first though."

Her father laughed. "And I wouldn't be mad if we ate, then you two left me at the hotel." He took his eyes off the road for a second, pleading first silently with his wife, then openly. "If two hours of chauffeuring you women doesn't earn me a pass from shopping, I don't know what will."

Mariah rubbed the back of his head, kindly. "But then who would carry our bags?"

She and Mina laughed as Jackson steered the truck into the far right lane and slowed to a crawl. The doors unlocked with a heavy thwump as he pretended to kick them out.

"Okay, okay," Mariah laughed, "you get a pass."

Mina chuckled at her parents teasing before turning her full attention to her phone. She kept up with life back at school and Sara's adventures visiting her grandparents, through messages that lit up her phone every few seconds.

The world of DRB High School was same stuff, different day.

But, Sara's exact message, Jess iz pissy & my life sux rt now, made her laugh out loud.

Funny, because hours later the sour Jess that Sara had griped about in no less than twenty-five text messages, was replaced by a remarkably chilled one. Mina wasn't sure if it was the ocean air or the truce making Jess bearable and even fun. As she hung out with Jess and Sara in the hallway of their hotel, she didn't care.

Their laughter echoed down the empty hall and for the second time that night Mina reminded herself 1) Sara was the real reason Mina bothered to put up with Jess, and 2) despite Mina's initial skepticism, Jess was taking the truce to heart. Both reasons were why the three of them were in the hallway of the hotel, putting the finishing touches on Mina's door.

Technically, only Mina and Sara were decorating the door with miscellaneous, hand-crafted Blue and Gold paraphernalia. Jessica sat on the floor cross-legged, her back against the door of the room across from Mina's, making fun of Mina's bad drawing and Sara's inability to tape anything straight. The Blue Devil heads, the blue megaphone with Mina's name on it in gold glitter, and the poster, Blue Devils Chicks Rock!, all slanted exactly the same way to the left, as if the hotel itself was on an angle. The girls burst out laughing each time Sara added a new piece. Even Mina's mother's warning to "keep it down" hadn't killed their giggling.

Each time, Sara thought she'd finally gotten it right.

Each time, Mina and Jessica's new fit of sniggling announced she'd failed.

With the last sign in hand, Sara approached the door, determined. She thrust the sign forward for a practice run.

Mina stood next to Jessica, watching. They sniggered under their breath as Sara stepped back, eyed the door, moved forward again, stepped back, eyed, moved forward.

"That's gonna be the new dance," Mina said. Making up her own tune she sang, "Step back, eye the door, move forward. Step back, eye the door, move forward."

Jess joined her. They added a hand clap to their simple ditty.

Sara waved them off. "I've got it this time," she declared, grabbing the tape from the floor. She advanced on the door one last time, held the poster with her knee and tore off a few pieces of tape before dropping the tape dispenser. She worked quickly to tape the poster's four corners, added two pieces on the sides for extra security then stepped back. Her arms folded in a triumphant, "there."

"Wait . . . wait . . . I think she has it," Jess said, her voice full of drama.

Mina abruptly ended her singing. She and Jessica tilted their heads as if they were watching a bowling ball's slow, off-kilter cruise to the pin. They stared at the last poster, a collage of cheer pictures. There was no white space on the board. The mass of mixed photos, upside down, sideways and every which way was so busy, it was hard to tell if the poster was straight.

Grinning, Sara waited on their judgment.

"It's . . ." Mina squinted, frowned. "I think it's . . ."

Mina's eyes focused on the poster once more then looked down at Jess, who was also concentrating. Their confused faces met for a second and then they chorused, "Slanting to the right, now," before giggling hysterically.

Sara harrumphed, but as she'd done all night, took their criticism in fun.

She gazed over her handiwork then at her sister and Mina, who were laughing it up, before fluffing her ear-length curls and declaring, "Well, just so you guys know. I totally did all the crooked stuff on purpose."

Mina and Jess gave one another an "un-huh, right" eyebrow raise and laughed more.

"So I've finally found something you suck at," Jess teased. "Sara the easygoing, perfect Johnson twin who can pick up any sport by just thinking about it, needs a ruler just to put up a sign straight."

"Don't hate me because I'm unique." Sara put her nose in the air and announced, haughtily, "Straight is so boring."

Mina gathered up the mess they'd made with all the paper and tape and dropped it into a small black knapsack. She threw the bag over her shoulder. "Okay. Now to your room." She locked arms with Sara as they made the short trip, three doors down. "We'll be so fashionable. The only two doors designed by Miss Sara Johnson of the DRB."

"You'll be known as The Angler in the interior design circles," Jessica said. She pushed herself off the floor and trailed behind them.

"Who would like an Angler original?" Sara asked, addressing an imaginary crowd.

Mina and Jess jumped up and down, raising their hands, shoving one another as they tried to get their hand seen through the "crowd."

"Well then, let me go get my stuff," Sara said, before disappearing into the room.

Jessica plopped back down on the floor. Mina stationed herself across from Jess, her back against the wall. There was an uncomfortable pause, neither of them sure how to fill the silence without their mediator.

For so long, Jess and Mina's relationship had been that of hunter and prey. Like a baby gazelle instinctively understood the nearby lion was his natural enemy, Mina had learned long ago to give Jessica a wide berth.

Finally, she took a small inhale and waited for Jess to diss something—her shirt, shoes, hair, crafting talents, cheer talents or the way she breathed. Usually everything was fair game.

Her breath came out in a snort of disbelief when Jessica said simply, "I'm sooo glad spring break is finally here."

She leaned her head back on the door. Her eyes closed, making her dark face a mask of serenity.

Mina ogled her for a full ten seconds, marveling both at the fact that Jess was making small talk and how many features Jess shared with Sara, despite having night and day complexions. They had the same nose and facial shape. And without the clipped, bossy tone in her voice, Jess sounded a lot like Sara.

Still, as casual as Jess was, Mina chose the safest conversation route, "Yeah. Me too," deciding to let Jessica lead the conversation.

Jessica's eyes fluttered open. She stared at the ceiling a few seconds before lifting her head. Her fingers raked thoughtfully through her weave, which was straight, for the day. "I would say I'm looking forward to summer but . . ." Her voice trailed off into a pregnant pause. When she spoke again, her nose wrinkled and she spit the words as if she were ridding her mouth of a bad taste. "My summer's shot. My parents are making me and Sara get jobs this summer."

Mina nodded, knowing instinctively that Mari-Beth Linton wouldn't be working this summer, which meant Jess would be left out of a lot of country-clubbing. Unable to help herself, Mina decided to bright-side it. "You know, it would be cool to work at Seventh Heaven in the mall. You guys should try and work there."

Jess snorted softly and shook her head. Her voice was more amazed than annoyed. "You seriously try and find the good in everything. Don't you?"

"I'm just saying, their clothes are hot and they have a DJ—it's probably like working at a nightclub," Mina said, unapologetic about her sunny optimism.

"I saw a cute pair of walking shorts in there last week," Jess said.

"Oooh, were they pink and green?" Mina asked. As Jess nodded she gushed. "Those *are* cute. See, if you worked there you'd get a discount."

"True," Jess said, without much excitement.

Sara popped out of the room at that instant. "Ready," she announced loudly, dropping a sack full of decorations on the floor. "What are you guys talking about?"

Mina busied herself poring through Sara's décor goodies as she answered, "Summer."

"Soon to be known as the end of our childhood," Jessica said, a sigh in her gloomy proclamation.

There was no misery in Sara's voice as she guessed at the root of Jessica's sadness. "Yup. We've gotta earn our keep around the Johnson ranch this summer."

"If only we actually did have a ranch," Jessica snorted.

Mina happily suggested Seventh Heaven again then joked, "I mean, the thought of having a discount by association at the mall's hottest store never occurred to me." She cut her eyes at both girls then popped them innocently. "I mean *never*."

Even Jessica laughed at the wink-wink hint.

Lying in bed later that night, or early the next morning, depending on how you looked at it, Mina thought about the evening and wondered if it had been real. She'd had such a good time. Her arms—buried under the hotel's thin sheet, a squeezably soft down blanket and a warm comforter—broke out in a million goose bumps at the admission.

Fun. I had fun with Jessica Johnson, her mind whispered as it drifted off into a dreamless sleep.

Drug Free

"Never sprung, huh?"
—Jay-Z, "Who You Wit II"

Thursday evening, Kelly and Angel walked along the quiet, empty street of her gated community, flush with McMansions and sculpted green lawns. She marveled at the way Angel fit in wherever he was. He was as easy and confident here as he was on the cracked pavement of The Cove's basketball courts, which were always surrounded by spectators, young and old.

Kelly secretly checked him out, playing her own game of Can Anyone Tell He's An (Ex) Drug Dealer? As always, she lost. If Angel were on that crazy game show where the contestant had to pick which person was in what profession, that contestant would lose. Angel had on a pair of dark-wash denim jeans that hung loose, but not baggy. They gave the impression that he was skinnier than he really was. The multicolored striped polo was the kicker that made him look so normal, in Kelly's opinion. Angel's caramel complexion against the shirt's vivid orange, yellow, and dark blue stripes was pale, but already taking on the soft glow of being in the spring sun, like maybe, just maybe, he'd been to a tanning salon recently.

No, she finally admitted to herself, no one would ever pinpoint Angel as a kingpin, or whatever he once was in the drug game. He blended in like a chameleon. At least he did as long as he didn't have the Muscle Twins with him, the two bodyguards who shadowed him seemingly twenty-four hours, except now and the other time Angel had come to Kelly's house. And, Kelly assumed, when he was in school. Now, Angel joked with Kevin, Kelly's eleven-year-old brother, about the prospect of him having to shave one day if he stayed on the Folger's Way swim team.

Kevin liked Angel and he took the jokes in stride, even teasing back. They seemed to have forgotten Kelly was there, giving her a chance to absorb the scene. Kevin and Angel had identical caramel complexions and shared similar features, small noses, smiling eyes— gray for Kevin, hazel for Angel. And wavy brown hair with a hint of red when the sun hit it—both kept it short, except Angel's was a little longer on top, his curls thick and swirling.

It hit Kelly that the three of them probably looked like siblings to people passing. Ninety-five percent of Folger's Way residents were white. Hers was the lone Latino family and there were two black families. No doubt, anyone driving by who recognized "the mixed-looking girl" would wonder where she'd picked up a second brother. On the swim and tennis teams, Kevin was better known in Folger's Way than Kelly.

They neared the community's clubhouse and Kevin gave Angel a pound before sprinting the last few yards to some teammates.

Angel waited for Kelly to catch up to him. His smile lit up his entire face as he called out, "Hurry up, nenesita."

"Well you two left me behind," Kelly grumbled playfully.

Angel stretched out his hand and she took it. A warm ribbon of pinpricks ran from her hand up her arm. She wondered if he could feel it.

They walked into the clubhouse, passing by the attendant who waved Kelly in, one of the few people who recognized Kelly by face— or more likely as Kevin Lopez's sister—and took a seat on the bleachers facing the pool.

Only a few parents littered the bleacher. The coach discouraged but didn't prohibit spectators during practice or trials.

Sitting side-by-side on the bleacher, with no space between them, Kelly and Angel could hardly be called spectators. Angel turned to look at her. Though Kelly kept her face looking out at the Olympic-sized pool, she wasn't paying attention to a thing going on in front of her.

"So, did you let any other dudes get at you since you blew me off?" Angel's eyebrow cocked and he paused, giving Kelly a chance to answer. But she took the fifth and held her peace. He chuckled softly. "I'ma take that as a yes. It's cool though, you with me now. Right?"

Kelly's earnest laugh rang out, echoing. She covered her mouth and lowered her chuckle. "First of all, you're dead wrong. I wasn't dating anyone." She almost admitted he was her first boyfriend to begin with, but didn't. She teased him, "And second, you called me so much that if I was seeing someone else you would have run him off."

Angel laughed. "Good." His face turned serious, reminding Kelly how quickly he could move from one emotion to the other. "What's up, mami? You finally gave in, so you obviously feeling a brother. Are you saying if I hadn't called to say I gave up dealing you wouldn't have let me get back with you?"

Kelly's eyes narrowed. "Are you trying to tell me something?"

Angel appraised her as if trying to read her thoughts, making Kelly shift nervously. She cleared her throat, waiting.

"No," Angel said after a tense few seconds. "I gave it up like I promised. It just trips me out how you so pressed about something I don't even do around you."

Kelly started to object but Angel defused the argument he saw coming by knocking knees with her. "It's all in the wind, mami. I was just trying to see where your heart was. It's swazy." He chuckled. "I'm drug free."

Kelly wondered aloud, "So what did your uncle say when you told him?"

"He pissed," Angel said, in a tone Kelly recognized immediately.

That's all he was going to say about that. She wanted to press further. Was there some ritual Angel had to go through to get out of the game, like when people get jumped into a gang? Or did she watch too much TV?

Her shoulders shook as she laughed silently.

"What's so funny?" Angel smiled.

"Nothing. It's just . . . you're always so secretive about that. But then you expect me to tell you the truth all the time," Kelly admitted.

"You think you want to know everything, but you don't. Trust." Angel glided his fingers over the back of Kelly's hand and dipped his fingers between hers. The two of them stared down at their hands, lost in thought.

"Can I ask one more thing?" Kelly said. Her heart beat faster as she anticipated Angel's no. He surprised her by nodding yes. "Is everything okay at home? I mean you didn't get kicked out or anything, right?"

"Naw, nothing like that." Angel knocked knees with her. "What, you think I'm Mafioso?"

Kelly giggled, embarrassed. *Uh, yeah, I do,* she thought to herself.

"Look, I was doing my uncle a solid. Now . . . you know, he can handle his business and I'm gon' handle mine." Angel flashed a smile, then knocked shoulders. "So, what's up for the weekend?"

Without hesitation, Kelly shared her plans to head to O.C. with Jacinta and Lizzie, the next day. Angel was amused and surprised and told her so. "Where this bad chick come from? *You* sneaking out?"

"Please, like you weren't the one who turned me bad."

Angel threw his hands up in surrender. "Un-ah, don't put that on me."

They shared a soft, couples laugh, as Kelly turned her hand over and took his hand in hers, loving how the blood immediately raced to her fingers.

THAT'S WHAT'S UP!   9 5

"So what would happen if I showed up in O.C. tomorrow night?" he whispered, his mouth tickling her ear.

"Where would you stay?" Kelly frowned.

"Don't worry about all that. You want me come down there?"

"I do but . . ." Kelly turned to look Angel in the eye. "Would you come by yourself? You know Jacinta and Raheem . . ." Kelly wasn't sure what to say about them.

"Those two don't know what they want," Angel snorted. "They were just together last weekend." Angel laughed as Kelly's eyes widened. "Oh, your girl didn't tell y'all that?"

"She did . . ." Well technically she hadn't. But Kelly figured Cinny had her reasons. "But I mean she said they argue a lot too."

"Okay, *argue*," Angel laughed. "Maybe they do. But not all the time."

Kelly knew what he was trying to say. But Jacinta seemed determined to keep things off with Raheem and Kelly respected that. She shook her head. "Don't come to O.C. if you're going to bring Raheem. I don't want to be the one who starts something."

Angel's lips tightened.

"So you gon' put Raheem and Cinny over me and you?"

A different type of heat crept up Kelly's neck. She swallowed hard, as if that would cool her down. At first, she and Angel had been the reason Jacinta and Raheem argued. Now it was the opposite.

Talk about your doomed connections, Kelly thought, glumly.

But just as quickly as he'd gotten angry, Angel changed again. He leaned back, his elbows on the bleacher behind him. His low speaking forced Kelly to swivel on the bleacher to face him. "It's cool, you want have your little girls' weekend in O.C." He grinned, leaning up, close to her face. "No boys allowed, huh?"

Kelly smiled, relieved. "No boys allowed."

Except JZ, Brian and Todd.

Cliiiiccckkk

"Don't look back at a new direction."
—Jordin Sparks, "Tattoo"

While Kelly and Angel canoodled at the pool, in O.C. Mina stared at the TV and it stared back at her. She had no idea what she was watching. She looked down at her cell phone, willing it to ring with news of the first outing.

When would the huge mass-texting that Sara had told her about, begin?

Last night Jess had bragged that the whole simul-text was her idea.

"All the right people will know where to come hang out," Jess had said, openly proud, as if she'd invented text messaging. She'd gone on to explain that she and the rest of the Glams would also be capturing Extreme moments with their picture phones and digicams and texting the best ones around.

According to Jess, this spring break would live on like a mobile scrapbook, serving as people's wallpaper forever.

As long as forever meant until the next hot photo came along, Mina had thought but kept to herself. She changed her cell phone's wallpaper whenever she was bored. She was doing it now as she waited for the message . . . any message that got her away from the torturous every-dayness of the close, boxy hotel room she shared with her parents.

Mina punched buttons on her phone, stamping away her boredom by cruising through her photo library for the millionth time. She thought about the text to come, wondering where tonight's big blowout would be. This was her first official event as an Upper. She'd downplayed her excitement last night but she was wound up as tight as a yo-yo right about now, bursting to get into the middle of the spring break madness.

She flipped her cell phone open, checking to make sure it was on.

"I'm tripping," she muttered, but triple checked that the phone had a signal (just in case) before quietly snapping it shut.

It was six o'clock and her phone hadn't emitted a peep yet.

Her heart skipped as she wondered if she'd been left out of the loop. Every DRB High Upper was right now, as she sat bored to tears, out getting their party on. She knew it. Jess's ultimate revenge, dangling the carrot in front of her only to swipe it and take a huge bite as soon as Mina went to touch it.

She'd be forced to head to dinner with her parents, nothing short of torture now that O.C. was crawling with DRB Uppers and the Blue Devils cheer squad.

She swung her legs off the bed and onto the floor, sitting erect as if a signal had sounded that only she could hear. Her father glanced quizzically over the top of the paper at Mina for a second before burying his head again.

Mina's knee began a jittery tap. She flipped the phone open again and just as she considered texting Sara, the cell vibrated in her hand. She opened it, stopping the thin buzzing tingling up her wrist.

The cavalry has arrived, she thought as she looked down at the message:

mt n lot in 3 mins goin 2 Guidos

Within fifteen minutes, Mina, Sara, Kim and Joss were making their way slowly through the crowded restaurant. Every few steps, one of them stopped and chatted with someone before resuming the crawl toward the booth gauntlet.

As far as Mina could figure, the hostess, in a vain attempt to keep the students in one area of the restaurant—and presumably out of the way of any non-Blue Devils customers—had sat all fifty people on the left side of the pizzeria, squeezed into seven booths. Some of the booths had too many people, several only a few—most people stood in the aisle between the two sets of booths, three per side, or hung over them.

One mega U-shaped booth sat at the end of the gauntlet, overflowing with people.

Mina stared agape at the brimming pizza joint.

If anyone ever needed proof that the Uppers were the real, honest-to-God mother of all cliques, an odd assortment of anyone deemed popular, there it was in 3-D at Guido's Pizza—the beachfront twin of Rio's Ria. Among the crowd was the student government president; captains of the baseball, soccer, lacrosse and football teams; a few from the theater set; and the "It's Academic" crew and members of the Geek Squad, the school's savviest techies.

If there had been any customers there before who were O.C. regulars, they were either long gone or racing to pay their check to get out of Dodge. Guidos was bona fide Blue Devils territory.

In the very first booth, Mari-Beth Linton held court, flanked by Jess and Simone. The other four Glams were packed into the other side of the booth, the ultimate ladies-in-waiting, ready to jump when the Queen said so.

Kim and Joss stopped at the booth to talk to Mari-Beth. Mina waved absently to Jess and was surprised when Jess threw her hand up in a casual hello. She and Sara milled through the crowd, hugging, waving and joking their way to the booth Cassidy was holding for them.

It was the last booth before the mega U-booth.

"We already ordered a pepperoni pizza," Cassidy yelled over the din. "Is that cool?"

Wide-eyed, Mina nodded, less in answer to Cassidy than at the sight of the newly designated Blue Devils section of Guidos. She fought and lost the battle to hide the awe that took root when the full scale of it hit. She was in the middle of all this, not an invited guest or bystander, but one hundred percent a part.

An insane urge to giggle assaulted her.

She wanted to grab Sara's arm and ask, "Am I really here? Or is this one of those real-feeling dreams?"

She hated real-feeling dreams. The kind where your entire body is so invested in the dream you're convinced that it's happening, until you wake up and realize it's not. They were worse than a mirage. She almost always emerged from those dreams angry and near tears that it was all a dream.

She'd dreamed a scene like this dozens of times. If it wasn't real she was going to have one doozy of a fit in the morning.

Sara knelt, her back to the table, talking to some of their squad mates in the booth behind them. Needing to share her amazement with someone, Mina leaned up as far as the table allowed and hollered over to Cassidy, "Can you believe this?"

She figured if anyone could relate it would be Cassidy, a fellow Junior Varsity squad mate turned Select Varsity. A few months ago they'd been the grunts doing all the work for pep rally and games. Now they were cooling out with the Varsity captain—on an elite competitive squad at that.

It was beyond wild.

Cassidy obviously agreed. She grinned as her head tick-tocked back and forth.

Mina openly marveled at every booth, craning her neck and turning in the seat to look behind her. Her eyes swept the room. She ticked off the Uppers she knew personally and those she only knew indirectly. Finally, her eyes stopped at the mega booth just behind Cassidy. It had gone from overflowing with people to only five. Her mouth went dry at the sight of Craig, laughing it up just inches away.

She stared, daring herself to look until he looked back.

What would she do if he looked over? Wave? Snarl? Roll her eyes?

Craig had publicly tongued down Kelis at a party, making Mina the fool du jour. Then he'd proceeded to dump her, abruptly, in the middle of the hall at school when she wouldn't up and forgive him on the spot. Yet Mina always felt like crawling under a rock when she saw him, as if she'd been the one who did wrong.

Every time she tried to muster the righteous indignation that should have accompanied the memory of their messy breakup, all she ended up feeling was a twinge of regret that things had ended so badly. She hated being hated.

Secretly, she longed for her and Craig to be frenemies, if nothing else. She could live with that. But the thought of making the first move to bury the hatchet sent a jolt to her heart. She reasoned, if any burying of the hatchet was going to be done, Craig should be doing it. After all, he'd have to remove it from her back first.

And there it was, for the first time—anger, hot and heavy on her chest.

Craig was the dogger, she was only the doggee. He should . . .

Craig flicked the rim of his hat up and Mina could see the full handsomeness of his light brown face—chiseled jaw and nose and slanted eyes just like Pharrell. He and the producer/artist could be related. Mina could barely listen to a Pharrell song without feeling a fizzle of anxiety and bitterness in her stomach. Craig's eyes narrowed to slits as he laughed along at a table-wide joke.

He was such a jerk.

But a cute one, she had to admit.

Their well-circulated breakup story hadn't tainted his reputation any. He'd gone through two other girlfriends since then. Not that Mina was counting.

She forced her eyes away before Craig noticed her, losing her solitary game of chicken.

They'd been doing a good job of pretending the other didn't exist. It might be bad luck to break the silent pact. She joined Sara's conversation.

By the time the pizza arrived, the table had gone through four rounds of visitors and she'd lost track of where Sara, Cassidy or Kim were. It didn't matter. For every person that hopped up and moved on, another moved into their spot. She was never without four or six people at the table to talk to and another half dozen at the one behind her.

Next thing Mina knew, Simone Simmons was next to their table. She shooed people out of the way, clearing a tiny space around her. "Cliiiccckkk," she shouted, swishing her straight, black hair and positioning her camera at the booth Mina was leaning over.

All the other Glams, except Mari-Beth, pulled their cameras out too. They each chose a spot along the gauntlet between the booths and began snapping.

Kim, who was on her way back to the table, scrambled over to Mina and pulled out her cell. "Come on, Mina."

"What?" Mina asked, as everyone around her scuttled into random groups.

"Every time they yell 'click,' jump into a picture or take one with your cellie." Kim held the cell up to capture them and the baseball player sitting with Mina, squeezed in. Another dove over the table to get into the shot. His foot skidded past the pizza on the table, right into their server's elbow, sending a whole tray of drinks to the floor.

He offered up a half-hearted "my bad," but the server was already muttering and picking up the plastic cups. She stalked off to replenish the drinks as the photo groups broke up and went back to their table-hopping.

Mina noticed that the server picked up fast—sure to avoid the Blue Devils' section whenever her super-server senses told her a photo op was on the horizon.

Kim got up and moved to the other side of the table. She nibbled on a slice of pizza as she moved over to let Chuck, her boyfriend, sit down. Giggling, she caught Mina up on what was happening several booths away.

Drunk with the vibe, Mina chomped on a slice of pizza, nodding along to the juicy bits Kim doled out.

This was exactly what she thought it would be like to be an Upper. It was friggin' awesome.

She scooted over when Bo, a Varsity football player and former crush, slid into the booth beside her. She and Bo had a little flirt thing going on earlier in the school year, but he was with Kelis now. Mina was surprised, but it seemed like they really liked each other.

A little into himself, Bo was dark skinned and hot-bodied fine.

"Hey Bo," she said, purposely dialing it down from flirt to buddy. She didn't need any more drama with Kelis.

Even through the heavy scent of garlic in the pizzeria, Bo's Irish Spring soap smell tickled Mina's nose. He helped himself to a slice of pizza. "What up, Mina?"

Mina exchanged a raised eyebrow with Kim and they laughed. "Hungry much?" Mina teased.

Chuck gave Bo a pound. "Wassup, dawg? You better lay off the mozz. Coach will pitch a bitch if you come into tryouts out of shape."

"Man, please," Bo said through a mouthful of pizza. He stood up and pulled up the polo that hugged his well-toned body. "See this six-pack? Your boy is ripped."

There were a few hoots of approval from the table beside them.

Mina admired his abs slyly, sharing a sneaky giggle with Kim. They both exploded into laughter as Mina looked down at a text from Kim that said, "hot hot hot."

Bo gave Chuck another pound and sat back down, beaming. Still sniggling, Mina asked, "Is Kelis coming down?"

"Naw. You know how hard it is for y'all fresh fish to roll with the big dogs," Bo said, every bit as arrogant as Mina remembered him from the summer. It was one reason why things never went beyond a crush for her.

Some people are so much cuter when they never talk, she thought, hoping Bo would move on.

"You know you probably wouldn't be down here either if you weren't on Select," Bo pointed out. He draped his arm on the back of the booth, closing the space between him and Mina. "No license, no chaperone, no road trip."

He put his fist out for some dap from Chuck, who was only half listening but still automatically touched fists with his teammate.

Mina rolled her eyes. "Not like we can help that we can't drive yet."

Bo lowered his voice and leaned his head in close to Mina's ear. "So, if you're on Varsity next year who you picking for your Blue Devil bro?" he asked, referring to the cheerleaders' Big Brother/Little Sister program.

All the Varsity cheerleaders "adopted" two football players. They decorated their locker on game day, left notes of encouragement, candy or other tokens of support.

"JZ," Mina said without hesitation.

Bo snorted. "Dag it's like that? You didn't even think about it."

Mina laughed. "You know Jay is my boy."

"Alright, well who else?" Bo laughed. "I know you not gonna say Craig. Not after he straight dogged you."

Mina's face burned.

Bo's voice got megaphone loud. "Craig!"

The people sitting at the mega booth with Craig looked Bo's way.

Mina's heart leapt. She slunk down in the seat, the prospect of dying of embarrassment very real. She tugged at Bo's arm as he bellowed Craig's name once more.

Craig looked up from the mega booth, smiling. "What up, B?" he yelled.

Bo motioned him over.

Mina watched, horrified, as Kim and Chuck chose that moment to leave the table.

"What are you doing?" Mina scream-whispered, not sure if she was talking to Kim or Bo.

She searched the gauntlet. The aisle was full of people, most with their backs to Mina's booth. She wondered where Sara, Cassidy, anyone was.

Craig, tall, lanky but sculpted, stood at their table. He didn't seem to mind that it was elbow-to-elbow people and he was being bumped and nudged right up against the table's edge. He and Bo exchanged a soul shake as Mina tried to disappear into the cheap upholstery of the booth. Penned in between Bo and the wall, she squirmed uncomfortably. Her bare calves squelched an ugly *brrrt* against the seat.

"Your girl here still jonesing for a little Craig juice," Bo said. "You must be dat man."

Mina felt like smacking the idiotic grin off Bo's face, but her eyes froze on Craig, taking a seat where seconds ago Kim had been snuggled up with her boyfriend.

The room was suddenly unbearably hot, burning Mina's throat and face. She sipped automatically from her soda, feeling incredibly alone with no one from the clique to have her back. No one was more surprised than her at the strength in her voice when she said, thickly, "Whatever, Bo. You're rummin'."

A flash of confusion crossed Bo's face, but quickly vanished as he challenged her. "Didn't you say you were gonna choose him as your Blue Devil Bro?"

"I never got to answer you," she corrected him. "You called Craig over before I said anything."

Her chest loosened a bit, as she defended herself. She allowed herself a moment of relief and chanted *this isn't so bad* in her head.

"What up, Mina?" Craig flashed a big, pretty smile that had once had the power to make Mina's knees wobbly. Now she just felt uncomfortable, like someone who had walked into the wrong room and couldn't backpedal out fast enough.

Her eyes fluttered downward. "Nothing."

Craig acted like they talked all the time.

Mina's head swam with the million and one things she'd been wanting to say to him, but didn't dare.

Determined to be the comic relief in the unfolding soap scene, Bo taunted, "Alright. Well who then?"

Mina scowled, for a second forgetting what Bo was talking about. "I don't know who else," she snapped when she recalled the original conversation that had brought Craig over.

"Oh you wouldn't pick me?" Craig asked, his eyes doing that thing where it seemed like he was looking into her mind.

She squirmed, determined not to let his charm unnerve her.

I have a boyfriend, I have a boyfriend. I don't care what Craig thinks anymore, she chanted in her head until some of the anger she'd felt earlier returned. "Now why would you want the jock ho to be your little sister?" Mina pierced him with a look, meeting his gaze for the first time. She resisted the urge to fold her arms and taunt, "Huh? Why Craig? Why? Huh?"

There was a little hiss from Craig, who never stopped grinning, as he said, "Man, I was just trying . . ."

"To dog me out?" Mina asked, boldly.

"Basically, yeah," Craig admitted.

Bo howled at that. "Son, you too honest." He put his fist out across the table and Craig touched his to it, his smile sheepish yet confident as ever.

It was the smile of someone used to being forgiven for everything, even for being a jerk, and the last straw that broke the back of the crush Mina had on him.

She rolled her eyes. "Shouldn't an 'I'm sorry' follow that?"

"Ohhh, little mama trying come hard," Bo said.

"My bad. I never apologized?" Craig laughed, confirming he knew good and well he hadn't.

Jessica stepped to the booth with a wide grin on her face.

"Cozy much, Mina?"

Quickly, Mina processed what the scene must look like: her squeezed so close to Bo they were joined at the thigh and side, and Craig oozing charm across the table. It probably looked like some bizarre dating game.

She pushed Bo away, shoving harder than playful allowed, as she said, "That's Bo smothering me."

Bo grabbed her in a bear hug. "You know how we roll, girl."

Jessica slid in next to Craig. She smiled knowingly at Mina. "Now, weren't we just talking about this, last night?"

The second Craig looked at Jess, waiting for her to explain, Mina shook her head furiously. She was afraid of what Jess, who was not above ad-libbing a conversation to start drama, might make up about their brief mention of Craig.

Last night Jessica had dared her to make nice with Craig. That was it.

She was relieved when Jess only offered, "I told you everything between you guys was swazy."

"I wouldn't say all that," Mina muttered.

Craig made sad eyes at her. "Why not? I apologized."

"Actually you didn't," Mina said, her right eyebrow arched practically to her hairline.

Craig nudged Jessica over, so he could get out, and walked over to Mina's side. There was a moment of musical chairs as Bo automatically got up and joined Jessica and Craig took Bo's spot next to Mina.

A tingle danced up her arm when Craig brushed against her.

Do not let him play hottie Jedi mind tricks on you, she screamed to herself.

"Okay, seriously, my bad for dogging you out," Craig said, his eyes flickering sincerity before playfully flirting again.

Losing interest as the scene turned more *Oprah* than *Jerry Springer,* Bo began a loud conversation with the mega-booth people Craig had left stranded. Jess watched, a crooked smile on her lips.

Mina pushed through the strange fuzziness settling into her brain. She and Craig hadn't been this close in months. Visions of where their relationship could have gone and where it had actually ended up flashed, before she abruptly faded the scenes to black and pointed out, "You know, saying 'my bad' isn't really an apology."

She scooted over as far as the wall allowed, putting an inch between her and Craig. With a mix of playfulness and dead seriousness, she added, "'My bad' means you were caught wrong and are admitting that you were caught."

Jessica groaned, "Oh my God. Only you would bother to point out the difference."

Jess's voice goosed her. So wrapped in Craig's web, Mina had almost forgotten they were in a crowded restaurant. She gasped under her breath as Craig closed the inch between them and said in his best, butter-wouldn't-melt-in-my-mouth voice, "Hey, Mina, I'm sorry for dogging you." He raised an eyebrow. "How's that?"

Jess clapped. "Now kiss and make up."

Mina's head snapped up, her eyes questioning why Jess would say something like that, then turned to face Craig, meaning to accept his apology. Her face collided with his as he held her chin and locked his lips over hers.

"Cliiiiccckkkkk," Jessica yelled. She pointed the camera at the kissing couple as the rest of the restaurant broke into a comical riot of people mugging for good shots.

Guilt Butterflies

"You got me tripping, stumbling, flipping, fumbling."
—Fergie, "Clumsy"

Mina's mind was in overdrive. Her lips tingled guiltily, but she made a show of pushing Craig away.

"Don't do that," she said weakly. She sat up straighter and nudged Craig away with her elbow, raising her voice. "Don't do that."

"Am I forgiven by the JV cheerleader voted phattest thighs?" Craig leaned in, pretending to peck at her lips again.

Mina reared back, bumping her head on the wall, sending Craig and Jess howling with laughter.

"You alright?" he asked, genuinely concerned. He smiled at her, sending guilt pangs to Mina's stomach. Then, as quickly as Jess, Craig and Bo had joined her at the table, they were gone, leaving Mina alone, a quiet island in the middle of the restaurant's escalating noise.

Sara bounced into the seat across from her. Grinning and out of breath, she prattled on. "Remind me that I'm not speaking to Andy. He took a picture of my butt crack." She cackled. "Things are so insane at Matt Patterson's table. He . . ." She waved at Mina. "Mi, are you listening?"

Mina shook her head. "Craig just kissed me."

Sara frowned, then laughed. "Ooh, you are so in trouble when Brian finds out."

Mina winced as a guilt pang pierced her chest.

"I didn't kiss him. He kissed me," she said, woodenly.

Sara chuckled and stuffed a piece of crust into her mouth. Crumbs flew as she said, "Let me know if that argument works out."

"He was just playing around," Mina said. She frowned in Craig's general direction. Not a word between them for four months and then he ups and kisses her.

Sara sprung up, disrupting her thoughts. "Let's go. Everyone's heading to the beach." She dug in her pocket, pulled out a few bills and laid them on the table.

Mina did the same and soon they were in the rowdy processional streaming out of Guidos and into the cool, breezy night. The moon lit up the beach. Within minutes, there was a party station in the center of the partyers, complete with speakers and several one-gallon milk jugs filled with something that definitely wasn't milk.

Surrounded by the squad, Mina sank back into satisfied fascination. They hadn't been on the beach ten minutes when Bo insisted on proving he could put the cheerleaders up in their complex stunts as easily as the girls stunted with one another.

"Shoot, if she can do it, I know I can," Bo boasted, thumbing toward Renee, a long-legged brunette with a hearty farm-girl build.

Renee's usual post was the back of the stunt, the strength and safety net if the stunt came tumbling down. She took considerable offense to Bo thinking her job was easy. She kicked sand at him and sprinted a few yards away when he tried putting her in a wrestling hold.

Mina snickered. It was typical male bravado. Guys like Bo spent just as much time laughing at male cheerleaders as they did proving they could do the same thing.

She watched as Bo knelt down and cupped his hands, beckoning for Cassidy, their tiniest flyer, to step in. Craig stood by his side, his hands in the air, mimicking a spotter.

"Okay. That is not how we put up a stunt," Mina said. She squinted at Craig. "And what are you supposed to be doing?"

She, Kim, Renee, Sara and Joss taunted the boys' inappropriate technique.

Cassidy made the sign of the cross, making the girls laugh harder, and stepped into Bo's hand. He hefted her up, cupping her tiny foot in his large hand. His muscles bulged as he demanded, "Come on, Cass, stand up, girl."

"No, bring me down," Cassidy said from above his head.

Seconds later her leg bent and she crumpled into his arms. Determined, Bo regrouped, trying again.

"Male cheerleaders are so much hotter than football players," Renee scoffed from the sideline. "A male cheerleader can lift one girl by himself, easily."

"Aw man, they're a bunch of punks," Bo muttered, even as he struggled to hold Cassidy in the air for longer than a few seconds. Cassidy nearly tumbled out of his hand and onto his head. "Alright, Mina, come on. I can do you," Bo declared.

"I'm bigger than Cassidy." Mina tossed her springy curls, teasing, "You can't handle this."

"Come on, C." Bo pulled Craig into the stunting. They imitated the cheerleaders' face-to-face stance and squatted so Mina could hop up. "Let's go, Mina. Want us to toss you?"

"Uh . . . hells no," Mina said, giggling along with the others. She stood, uncertain, in between the boys' knock-kneed squat. She placed her hands on their shoulders, started to hop into their hands then wagged her finger in Craig's face. "Keep your lips to yourself. Alright?"

Smiling slyly, he leaned in so only Mina could hear him. "Like you didn't like it."

Guilt butterflies fluttered in her belly and she hesitated.

"Come on, girl. I'm just playing," Craig said, then mimed zipping his lips.

Mina eyed him a second longer. She had no idea what that kiss had been about or why Craig had done it. She silently chanted Brian's name to keep her focus as she hopped into the first but not last disastrous stunt of the night.

Road Trippin'

"Let's make our move and get into a little something."
—Keke Palmer, "Keep it Movin' "

It's only a sleepover.

It's only a sleepover.

Lizzie mouthed the words over and over as she stood watch at the front door.

She peeped out of the side window panels, her body rigid with anticipation. The house's silence soothed her nerves, momentarily, as she repeated her mantra, "It's only a sleepover."

The muscles in her neck loosened and her shoulders relaxed until her mind kicked in its own reminder: A sleepover, over one hundred miles away . . . in a condo full of guys.

She smushed her forehead against the pane, pleading with her brain to not go there. The coolness relieved the heat burning through her face. She closed her eyes and took a few calming breaths, the same thing she did when she was preparing for an audition.

In a way, this was an audition. If she pulled off this caper she'd join the ranks of every teen who had ever successfully pulled one—a real whopper—over on their parents. It was the one role she'd never mastered because of that pesky inability to lie thing.

She chuckled bitterly, torn because as nervous as she was, as queasy as she felt, she was also excited.

Nausea rolled in a soft fluid wave.

Brian would be pulling up any second now. In a few hours, she'd be in O.C. spending the night with her crush.

A smile crept across her face and the wave of nausea rolled back out.

The truth was she could beg off, tell the clique the truth—she was scared of getting caught and in trouble. But she hadn't and wouldn't because Todd was completely cool if she chickened out. He'd told her so the other day when she admitted being nervous.

"You're a total rebel. That's hot," Todd had said, flashing his goofy grin at her. He was so cute, it made Lizzie's toes curl. Then he'd grown serious. "But, if you don't want to, just tell Cinny." He chuckled as he added, "I'll have your back when she goes off."

It made her want to go even more, knowing she didn't have to pretend to be something she wasn't, because she so wasn't a rebel. But she was ready to live a little.

Lizzie blew her hot breath on the cool window and drew a heart in the steam. She jumped when her cell phone bleated, the loud ring echoing in the silent house.

"Hey Mom," she said, her heart racing.

"Have you left yet?"

"Nope. Still waiting on Brian to drop me over to Cinny's." The half-truth slid out of Lizzie's mouth surprisingly easily.

"Well, Dad and I are going to the Inner Harbor tomorrow. Do you girls want to ride with us? We can pick you up from Jacinta's."

Lizzie's mouth went dry. She blanked out, brought back only by her mom's voice calling, "Lizzie? Did I lose you? Stupid cell . . ."

"No, I'm still here," Lizzie answered. "Umm, remember I told you we were going to the movies?"

"Oh, I thought that was tonight," her mom said. "Okay. Well have fun. Miss Jacqi's dropping you off on Sunday night?"

"I was sort of hoping that you'd let me stay since Mina will be back on Sunday . . ."

"Lizzie, honestly . . . the entire weekend away?"

"School's closed until Tuesday and . . ."

"Yes, but that doesn't mean you girls have to spend every second of the break together." There was a brief pause then her mom's hurried voice. "We'll talk about it Sunday. I need to take this call, honey. Have fun."

Just as Lizzie flipped the phone closed, Brian's Explorer pulled up. He blew the horn once. A back door opened and Jacinta popped out. But Lizzie already had the house door open. She grabbed her two bags—she'd majorly overpacked, worrying mostly about what pajamas to bring. *What do you wear to bed when your crush is in the next room?*

She was to the car before Jacinta made it to the sidewalk.

"Ready chick?" Jacinta beamed.

Lizzie only nodded. Her nerves were back in full force.

She'd been fine until her mom called. *What was it with parents? Did they have a sixth sense?*

"You okay?" Jacinta frowned.

"Fine." Lizzie took hurried inventory of the seating arrangement. JZ rode shotgun. Kelly was in the second row and Todd was in the third seat. He leaned his long torso over and folded the seat down so Lizzie could climb in the back.

"Come on back to the love shack," he teased.

Lizzie's cheeks burned.

Luckily, her legs did the work, ignoring her freaked-out mind. She stepped onto the running board, kneeled on the folded seat and climbed into the third row of the SUV.

Before she knew it, Jacinta was in, the door was shut and Brian was pulling out of her neighborhood.

"Liz-O, what up girl?" JZ called from the front seat.

"I think we're all insane," Lizzie blurted.

Kelly laughed. "We totally are."

"I don't mean any harm but I'm hungry," Jacinta said. "Brian, stop a chick at Five Guys or something."

"Naw, no stops until we get over the bridge," Brian lectured. The clique groaned and his fatherly tone went up a notch. "Look, otherwise we gon' end up stuck in traffic for days." He snorted. "Y'all better be chill."

He turned up the radio and the Go-Go blasted from the speakers.

"Okay, please not Go-Go for two full hours," Kelly yelled over the music.

"Yes, for two hours." Brian banged on the steering wheel in time to the drum beat.

"Why couldn't Mina date a guy from Atlanta or something," Jacinta joked.

"I know you not saying snap music better than Go-Go." Brian stared her down in the rearview mirror.

"Ay, y'all just stowaways on this trip," JZ said. "No requests allowed."

JZ and Brian exchanged pounds and Todd reached his entire body from the third row over the second to get a pound in.

Jacinta pushed Todd toward the backseat.

"Alright, White Chocolate, don't make me hurt you."

The Go-Go boomed and the clique continued to talk over it, as Brian handled the Explorer in the already growing traffic.

Lizzie threw out an occasional quip, but fear and excitement kept her mum and made her restless. She raked her hair, folded then unfolded her arms then finally gnawed at her thumbnail as the disses and jokes flew throughout the truck.

She leaned up behind Kelly, whose head kept peeking down.

"What are you doing?"

"Oh, Angel keeps texting me," Kelly said. She raised her voice. "Angel says what's up y'all."

"What's up, Angel," everybody yelled.

Kelly laughed. "Okay, technically he's only talking to Lizzie and Jacinta. I never told him we were riding down with you guys."

"Uh-oh, Kelly, you not truthing up to your boy?" Jacinta teased.

"How does he think you're getting there?" Lizzie asked.

Kelly shrugged. Angel hadn't asked and she hadn't told.

"I think I may have to find some new friends. You guys are crazy *and* a bad influence," Lizzie said.

"They rummin', Liz?" JZ yelled toward the back.

Lizzie chuckled. "Yeah, they're rummin'."

"JZ, that word is not hot," Jacinta said.

"Now, you rummin'. My word is hot to death," JZ said. He reached his hand back without turning around, and tugged at Jacinta's foot until her shoe slipped off. He dangled it out of the window pretending he was going to drop it. Jacinta's arms flailed over the seat as she tried pulling his arm back in. They scrambled for a few seconds before he reluctantly tossed the shoe onto the second row of seats.

"Oh, now you are rummin'," Jacinta said.

JZ's laugh was rich and deep. "Told you y'all would start using it."

Jacinta smacked at the back of his head.

Todd bumped knees with Lizzie, smiling ear to ear.

They both chorused, "They're rummin'," then laughed.

He held out a stick of gum. "Fresh breath, pact?" he asked.

Lizzie squinted. "Huh?"

He put his right hand over his heart. "I, Todd, pledge to keep my breath minty fresh the entire spring break in case Lizzie . . . ya know, wants to kiss me."

Lizzie's laughter was caught up in the beating of the music's drums. She nodded and reached for the gum, but Todd pulled it back.

"Now you," Todd said. "Say the oath."

She giggled as she tried to remember Todd's exact words. "I, Lizzie . . . pledge to . . ."

"Keep my breath minty fresh," Todd guided.

"Keep my breath minty fresh . . . the entire break in case Todd wants to kiss me."

"No, you have to say 'ya know' before the kiss part," Todd said, dead serious.

"My bad." Lizzie pretended to get serious. "In case Todd . . . ya know, wants to kiss me."

Todd slipped a stick of gum out of the wrapper, bit off half and held the other half in front of Lizzie's mouth. She opened wide and he placed the gum on her tongue.

He popped the gum happily. "Fresh pact oath."

"Fresh pact oath," Lizzie repeated, munching along, letting Todd's friendly blue eyes wash away her uncertainty.

Fun Hangover

"Break it off boy, cause ya got me feeling naughty."
—Rihanna ft. Sean Paul, "Break It Off"

Mina was no longer drunk from the vibe of last night's reckless abandon. The practice room, a plain square twenty-foot box with mats, was filled with a deafening silence as Coach Embry stabbed the stop button on the CD player.

The girls stared silently, waiting for the expected lecture.

Fear ran from Mina's chest to her sore legs as Coach Em gave her the crook eye.

She'd failed to hit the double down even one good time. Her head hung low against Coach Em's rant.

"Obviously, you ladies have forgotten what you're here for. This practice was a waste of my time." She fixed every girl with a steely piercing glare, stopping on Mina. "Care to explain why a stunt you'd *finally* gotten to an acceptable level now looks like . . . crap?"

It was the kind of question that required an answer. Yet Mina knew the real answer—she was dog tired and sore from last night—would only further frustrate Coach Em. And, admitting that her legs felt like lead and her head full of marbles was a sure enough death sentence for any further pre-competition partying.

Which may not be such a bad thing, she thought sullenly.

"Your arms are flying all over the place," Coach Em barked, still focused on Mina. "Kim almost lost an eye that time."

Kim gave Mina's lower back a sly, sympathetic pat. It sent Mina over the edge and she gulped over the lump in her throat, silently begging the tears not to follow.

The guys' clumsy technique and near spills had left her ribs bruised, and her legs were sore from balancing on their lopsided, shaky holds. Keeping her body tight in the double down made her muscles scream. She wasn't the only one sore or out of sorts, but she dared not point that out.

Coach Em took a huge breath, blew it out toward the ceiling then picked up her bag. She headed to the door and stopped. "Don't forget curfew is ten tonight." Her tone was flat. "Not a second later. No excuses."

She walked out, leaving the squad in stunned silence. Wise, since seconds later she popped her head back in the door. "Don't make me regret putting this team together, ladies. And Mina, prove me wrong . . . because I'm having serious second thoughts about choosing Freshmen for this squad at all."

With that she walked back out, for good.

The girls were somber as they headed their separate ways. But eight hours and a couple of power naps later, the tired sad sacks from that morning were gone. Freshly made up, sporting their cutest street clothes instead of spirit gear, the cheerleaders sat scattered in the near-empty, raised bleachers at the back of the arena among the other Uppers.

The bad practice was behind them.

The arena had six sections of bleachers, eighteen rows high. Even the first row of bleachers sat four feet off the ground. The DRB Uppers were so far away from the stage, nearly two football fields' length, they couldn't have made it more obvious they were not there for the performances.

There was a good crowd in attendance. Nothing like it would be for the main event, but the twelve-thousand-seat arena was a quarter full. People who had come to actually watch the Individual and Partner stunts sat in or milled around the floor seats, their gazes focused on the stage.

At one time, Coach Em had tried recruiting some of the girls to register for Individual or Partner stunts, but the idea of adding yet another practice onto their already full schedule appealed to no one. Tonight, they were just happy spring breakers, except Mina, whose anxiety over the double down built to a crescendo as she watched team after team perform the same stunt near perfectly.

As her squad mates talked over and around her, she fixated on the jumbo screen that gave her a better view of the stage.

Three girls took the blue-carpeted cheer floor. They wore black shorts, orange sleeveless polos and black and orange ribbons in their hair. When the music started they lifted and threw their flyer into various positions, quick-changing to the beat. Mina watched as the flyer went up smooth as oil, did the double twist that had Mina's stomach in knots, and then shot right back up in the air holding one leg behind her head.

She groaned. "I hope they're not in our division tomorrow."

"Who?" Sara asked.

Mina pointed to the stage. "She already doubled twice. Flawlessly."

Sara rubbed Mina's arm. "You'll be okay. Stop thinking about it."

"Easier said than done." Mina's eyes followed the stunt team until the music came to an abrupt end and they spirited their way off the stage.

"I know what will take your mind off it," Sara said. She nudged Mina with her elbow and pointed toward the arena doors. "Cutie at two o'clock."

Mina frowned. "What cutie?"

Sara sucked her teeth then took her hands and adjusted Mina's head in the right direction. "Brian's here."

Mina squinted through the darkened room until she recognized three tall shapes scanning the cavernous arena. The light from the hallway shone behind them enough for her to see it was definitely Brian, JZ and Todd. She smiled, then squealed when she saw three more figures come from behind the guys.

She stood up and clapped. "Oh my God!"

"Are you cheering for those girls that were just on the stage?" Renee asked. "They were amazing."

Mina laughed. "No, my girls are here."

Squeezing her way out of the bleachers, she speed-walked over to the clique.

Her screams of happiness were lost in the noise of the music as yet another partner stunt group launched into their routine. The girls talked over each other, everyone trying to get in a question or answer.

"How's the truce going?" Kelly sang.

Mina's answer was a dismissive, "Well, we haven't killed each other."

"Puh. I still can't even believe you trusting that girl," Jacinta said. And just in case Mina did not catch that Jacinta still hated Jessica she added a skeptical eye roll and pinched-mouth frown for good measure. Both disappeared when Mina bumped shoulders with her playfully.

"Only you would trust someone like her. Only you, Princess," Jacinta laughed.

"Is your mom here tonight?" Lizzie asked, scouring the arena anxiously.

"It's pretty crowded in here, huh?" Kelly asked.

Mina shook her head no and nodded to answer both questions.

"I'm starving. Your man refused to stop." Jacinta stuck her tongue out at Brian.

"Okay. First things first . . ." Mina put her hands on her hips. "What are y'all doing here? And how come I was clueless you were coming?"

There was a fresh round of cross-talking.

"It was Cinny's idea."

"We wanted to surprise you."

"Can you believe we snuck down here?"

"Uhh . . . no," Mina laughed, delirious with giddiness. The double down, the kiss, even the excitement of Guidos grew cloudy in the face of the girls being there.

Before they ever left the arena entrance she was caught up in every detail of their odyssey as rebel road-trippers. She wasn't sure if her racing heart was because of her excitement that her friends were there, fear at the thought of them getting caught, thrill that they'd risk major punishment for the Extreme (and her), or jealousy that she'd missed out on the ride down, full of dissing and apparently kissing (Go Liz).

"I've been having a good time with the squad," Mina admitted. "But it's nothing like kicking it with your girls."

She squeezed them together for a group hug.

"Don't go all soft on us, Princess," Jacinta fussed, shying away from Mina's embrace before letting herself be smothered by the four-way hug.

Brian tapped Mina on the shoulder.

"Can the driver get in on some of this?"

Mina turned and felt her feet leave the ground as Brian lifted her in his hug. She wrapped her arms around his neck, holding on for dear life then kissed him on the lips, savoring how full her heart felt to see him. For the briefest second, she'd been afraid to greet him, scared something inside her had changed and he'd be able to tell.

She was so happy to see him her heart was pounding as if it were trying to beat its way out of her chest.

"Thank you for bringing down my girls," Mina gushed.

"Man, your girls a trip." Brian shook his head. He placed Mina back down and mocked a girlish-nag. "Stop here, Brian. No, stop there."

They all trailed behind JZ and Todd, who had spotted the Blue Devil section.

Brian raised his voice. "Do I look like my name is Jeeves the Chauffeur?"

"Jeeves is a butler's name," Kelly informed him.

Mina laughed as Brian shoved Kelly's shoulder, making her trip over a cord.

Kelly made sad eyes. "Mina, promise that your next boyfriend will take orders better."

Mina held onto Brian's hand. "Okay. But I think I'm going to keep this one for a while."

Brian squinted down at her. "Oh, it's like that?"

"What?" Mina feigned ignorance. "I said I was going to keep you for a while."

She squeezed Brian's hand then blew him a kiss. He ducked from it, sending her and Kelly into a fit of giggles.

The clique wasn't there long before Mina suggested they head back to Brian's condo. She wanted to be totally in the middle of the girls' road trip adventure and invited Sara along.

This would be the greatest road trip story ever, even if they did get caught. It was the kind of gutsy stuff that legends were made of. The type of stories people in school would be talking about for years. "Remember when Jacinta, Kelly and Lizzie snuck down to the Extreme and . . ."

The buzz and whispering about it had already begun and had spread especially quick since the tale was accompanied by, "Don't tell anyone. They don't want it getting back to Mina's parents."

Clearly, "don't tell anyone" was the international code for, "tell everybody!"

Assured Brian would have her and Sara back in time to catch a ride to the hotel with Kim, Mina and the group made a loud exit out of the arena. Once they were settled in the Explorer, Sara immediately confirmed what Mina had been thinking.

"Man, everybody's talking about you guys."

"Why?" Kelly asked over JZ's loud grumbling about Mina taking shotgun.

"Just surprised that you guys snuck down here," Sara said. "You're frosh. Plus, everybody thinks you're shy, Kelly."

Kelly shrugged. "I'm used to that." She wrinkled her nose. "Why does shy have to mean totally unadventurous and boring?"

"I don't know. But you're sure not. Y'all are little rebel chicks," Mina said, every bit as proud as a momma bird watching her chicks on their debut solo flight. She turned in the seat to catch a glimpse of Sara's nodding head. "Did you see Mari-Beth's face?" Mina giggled wildly and imitated Mari-Beth's snitty pitch. "Wow, Kelly even *you're* on the sneak tip. You have more balls than I thought."

"Kelly's that woman," Jacinta crowed. "She try play all quiet but she's a down chick."

"Hey what about me?" Lizzie frowned. "I'm the truly quiet one. Aren't I down?"

"I was hoping the quiet thing was just an act," Todd quipped.

Jacinta snorted. "Well you gonna be all burnt because it's not. Liz is a straight-up good girl. Not like Mina and Kelly."

There was a whoop of disagreement from Kelly and Mina. They talked over one another denying they were anything short of angels.

"That's my girl. Bad to the bone," Brian hollered.

Mina rolled her eyes and bit back a grin. "Don't get it twisted, I'm still ninety percent good girl."

"Shoot, as long as there's that ten percent chance," Brian said, and put his fist toward the back for a pound from JZ.

JZ gleefully knocked fists with him.

"Leave it to me to get stuck with the pure good girl," Todd teased, shirking away from Lizzie's shove.

"All I know is, everybody was talking about it before we left tonight," Sara said. "You guys are going to gain some serious cred for this. You're like on some junior, senior level sneak tip." She chuckled.

"Freshman on the breakaway road trip . . . that's one for the DRB High books."

"I'm not claiming any titles until we get away with it," Lizzie said, anxiety edging into her voice.

Todd gave her knee a reassuring knock with his own, making her smile.

"Even if you don't, you guys still get cool points for coming all this way solo," Sara said.

The truck was silent for a moment, except for the music playing at mid-level, as the girls seemed to consider their newfound status. None of them cared about running in the Upper circle like Mina. Lizzie's focus was always her grades and her acting. Jacinta simply didn't care about being "in." And Kelly had transferred to Del Rio Bay High to get away from the pecking order lifestyle of elite McStew Academy.

But Mina saw it on their faces, they weren't exactly disappointed to hear that their peers were doling out props for their impulsive act.

Brian pulled the truck into a parking spot in front of a high-rise tower. Excitement filtered through the car as everyone commented on the tall building. They went from the elevator with the TV monitor playing CNN, to a twentieth floor, three-bedroom condo furnished as if it should be in a lifestyle magazine.

The carpet was thick and a light crème color so clean it seemed a sin to walk on it with shoes. Pictures of Brian and his parents were grouped in a simple collage on the wall across from the kitchen, black art was tastefully displayed throughout all the others.

It was obvious the Jameses either came to their ocean condo often or wanted it to feel just like home when they did come. The place looked and felt lived in.

Instinctively the girls roamed the entire place, commenting on Brian's mom's good taste, while the guys headed to the patio off the living room.

After giving herself the grand tour, Mina joined the guys. It was too dark to see much of the beach below. But the smells and sounds of the ocean overpowered her senses the second she stepped onto the balcony. She didn't have to breathe in the air, it simply sucked her into it.

That high up, the breeze from the water whipped her hair and chilled her bare calves and ankles. She put her arms around Brian and rooted her face into his shirt for warmth.

Lizzie and Sara came out to the balcony. They stared out into the blackness while Jacinta lingered back, choosing to stand in the sliding-glass doorway. Kelly stood beside her.

"Y'all know I have a thing about heights," Jacinta said, her voice shaky with fear.

JZ tugged her arm, but Jacinta snatched it away, bolting to the safety of the middle of the living room.

Mina admonished him. "No, Jay, for real. She was even afraid to sit on Sara and Jessica's trampoline."

Sara chuckled. "And that's not even ten feet off the ground."

"Are y'all talking about me?" Jacinta called, refusing to move back to the doorway.

"Just telling JZ to stop playing around," Mina said, like a mother calming a child.

"Alright, who down for a game of spades?" JZ announced.

Jacinta raised her hand. "As long as we're playing in here."

"Teams?" JZ asked. "I got you, Cinny."

"Me and you, Kelly?" Sara asked.

"I'm not very good, but I'll play," Lizzie said.

"I got you," Todd boasted. "We're gonna kick some beeeep beeeep."

Brian took a seat in one of the patio's chaise lounges and patted the seat.

Taking the hint she peeked her head into the doorway. "We're not gonna play, y'all."

The clique sat at the oak dining-room table, the smack talk already in high gear. JZ shuffled cards, doled out rules and boasted about his spades prowess. Mina closed the slider and happily joined Brian on the seat, leaning back on his chest, her short legs not even taking up the entire length of the chair.

She zipped her jacket and tried not to focus on the breeze and how chilly was quickly turning into cold. If they went inside they'd lose some privacy. Plus the sounds of the crashing waves was movie-perfect romantic. So what if her ears were *thisclose* to being ice cold and her fingers were following.

Reading her mind, Brian massaged her arms and fingers gently. The friction did its job and Mina's blood flowed to the cool spots.

"You know I was surprised when you asked to come over, right?" Brian said.

Mina loved the way his voice, above a whisper but lower than an inside voice, mixed with the sound of the waves below. It felt wrong to break up the rhythm so she only nodded.

The bass from his voice boomed against her back as he said, "I figured we were just gonna cool out at the arena." Mina felt his chest heave as he took a breath. She closed her eyes, not just listening but feeling every word he said. "That would have been alright. But I'm glad we came back here."

She nodded again, hoping he'd keep talking.

He wrapped his arms around her, settling his hands on her stomach.

"Would you have come back here if I asked you to by yourself . . . without Jacinta and them?"

He lowered his head, as if he were trying to look at her face, and his cheek rested against Mina's frigid ear. Their body heat mingled and her ear started to thaw. She shook her head no in answer to his question.

"Seriously, you have never been this quiet the entire time we've known each other."

Her soft chuckle joined his, then he picked up where he left off.

"So you wouldn't have rolled with me without your girls?" His fingers tapped at her belly, tickling. "Dag, you act like you can't trust me by yourself."

Mina shook her head no, again, took a breath and finally spoke. "It's not you I don't trust."

She sat up, threw her legs over the side of the chair and turned so they were facing each other. She paused when a loud exclamation of "Ohhh . . . you reneged!" and some light arguing came from inside.

Noticing that Brian didn't even turn to check on the clique's antics inside, she forced herself to do the same.

"It's me I don't trust." Her cheeks went warm as Brian grinned at her in that way she loved—his eyes and mouth smiling, making his face one big irresistible smiley. "See, that's why I don't trust myself. You be playing those hottie Jedi mind tricks on a girl."

She pretended to push herself up and move away but he pulled her back down beside him and her attempt at resistance was weak.

"For real, you know you're hot, don't you? Just admit it," Mina teased.

"Do I get more points for saying no or for being honest?"

His grin went from cute to devilish and cute.

Mina elbowed him in the gut. "You are not all that."

Brian scooped her up toward him and slid her onto his lap. "Yes, I am."

He kissed her before she could protest.

More arguing broke out inside and out of nowhere a music video blared from the TV. But Mina didn't hear a sound of it.

Her and Brian's kiss went from playful to purposeful and by the time his lips moved to her neck, nibbling gently, Mina had forgotten they were outside and that it was cold. Her entire body was feverish.

Neither of them heard the slider open or JZ's footsteps as he walked over and stood beside the lounge chair. His voice boomed, sending Mina out of Brian's lap like a sprinter out of the starting block.

"Ay Brian, what's the closest store, man?" He laughed at Mina's meteoric position change. "My bad. I didn't mean to bust your groove."

"You scared me," Mina mumbled. Her hands shook, from where she and Brian were taking things or from JZ's voice shocking her like a lightning bolt, she wasn't sure.

"What, you thought it was your moms?" JZ cracked up.

"There's a Seven-Eleven right next door and a grocery store across the street," Brian said, patiently.

Mina squinted inside to the living room.

"Y'all done already?"

JZ snorted. "Man, those dudes are cheating." He stepped back and repeated it inside the condo, snickering when Lizzie defended herself.

"I told you I didn't play well. I'm not cheating, just really bad at this."

"We were just gonna run and get some grub," JZ said. "Y'all want anything?"

Both Brian and Mina shook their heads.

"Is everyone going?" Mina asked. She downplayed the panic she heard in her voice by adding hurriedly, "It just seems like by the time y'all do all that you're going to have to take me back to the arena. Why bother?"

JZ took his cell phone out and looked at the time. "Well, Lizzie 'nem staying here, remember? Brian could take you and Sara back."

Mina's eyes crinkled with hurt. "Dag, Jay, just push me off the balcony if you're that pressed to get rid of me."

In two strides he was by her side, trying to put her in a headlock. "My bad, Mouthy Mi. I didn't mean it like that." He got the expected shove from Mina as she avoided his move. "But y'all have like an hour. We have time. It's gonna be a quick run."

He strode back inside. "Come on, we have time to hit the store."

Jacinta came as close to the slider as she dared, Sara and Lizzie peeking around her. "Mi, you don't want anything?" She smiled slyly. "Or, I guess you got everything you need."

The girls tittered.

Mina raked her hair nervously before waving them off.

Their girly ring of laughter was cut off as the front door shut behind them, leaving Mina alone with Brian, the waves and the loud music videos.

Brian stood up, took her hand and walked inside. He left her standing in the doorway as he busied himself turning down the TV.

"Man, they act like they're deaf," he muttered.

Mina's heart raced. She wasn't sure what she mumbled in response because all she heard was her brain screaming, *he's going to turn off the lights next and then start walking to a bedroom.* She stood frozen by the slider, her legs refusing to move any farther inside.

Realizing that she probably looked as frightened as she felt, she blinked a few times and fought off a high-pitched squeak as she said, "This is a really nice condo."

"Thanks." Brian cut his eyes at her and lowered his voice. "Want to see my room? It's even nicer."

His laughter filled the empty living room. He fell onto the pastel-colored floral couch, his body shaking from laughing. After a few minutes he sat up. "Mina, I'm playing. I'm not gonna jump you. Chillax." He stopped laughing long enough to sweep his eyes over her body approvingly. "Even though those phat thighs are like . . ." He shook his head and muttered "mmm, mmm, mmm" like he was talking about a bucket of juicy chicken thighs.

Mina smiled at the compliment but it felt frozen and phony. She looked like someone who'd just majorly overreacted in *Scary Movie X: The Date Movie* or some other campy B-movie.

Her heart galloped, but she moved slowly to the sofa, hoping her fingers would stop trembling by the time she reached it.

They didn't and Brian didn't let her off the hook about it. "You're shaking, for real." He shook his head, still chuckling.

Mina raised an eyebrow in irritation and Brian's laugh finally fizzled out, only to be replaced by his signature amused grin. It put

Mina at ease and there was a comfortable silence between them, filled by the television's low music.

She tucked her legs beneath her on the couch, grateful that her heart was slowing down and the awkward moment passed. She pretended to pout.

"You didn't have to laugh at me."

"I'm just tripping off you being straight scared of me," Brian said.

"No, you mean you're rummin'." Mina chuckled. She wagged a finger in his face. "Number one, I'm not scared of you." She met Brian's gaze, her confidence growing, but then fading for an instant as she admitted, "But you know we never really talked about . . . I mean . . . it's not like we . . ." Her eyes fluttered as she searched for the right words before settling on, "You know what I'm trying to say?"

He scowled. "No. Just say it."

Mina took a deep breath and let it filter slowly through her nose before continuing. "We never talked about . . . sex."

She whispered the word and it made Brian smile.

"Okay, what do you want to know about . . ." Brian whispered, "Sex."

"I don't want to know anything. But maybe you should know it ain't happening . . . tonight," she quipped.

Brian's eyes drooped in a sad, puppy dog way. "We're not? I thought for sure your eyes popping out of your head was a sign we were gonna."

He laughed wildly again, ducking as Mina swung one of the decorative pillows at him. He rebounded quickly and tugged at her, causing her to roll to his side of the sofa. She unfolded her legs and voluntarily hopped onto his lap.

She kissed him. He responded, darting his tongue in her mouth. They went on like that a few minutes longer, both taking great pains to keep the heat at bay.

It startled her when he pulled away and asked, "Do you remember what I said when we first started going out?"

Mina's brain froze. She had no idea what he was talking about.

"No games, just being straight up with each other," he reminded her.

She nodded, remembering how Brian had stepped to her one morning, asking her straight out if she was feeling him because he liked her.

His honesty was like woah. It caught her off guard that morning and still did most times.

"I'm just saying, that's me. That's how I do," Brian continued. "Just let me know what's up and I'll always do the same."

Mina was glad to hear Brian say that. But she still couldn't bring herself to make any comment about how ready or unready she was. Instead, she nodded and sank back into his arms, letting their kisses do the talking.

Madness in . . . 5 . . . 4 . . . 3 . . . 2 . . .

"Do you feel like a man when you push her around."
—The Red Jumpsuit Apparatus, "Face Down"

There was a millisecond of quiet.

Then the final echoing of the canned voice-over exclaiming, "Bluueee Devils!" was replaced with screams of the Blue Devils fans.

On stage, Mina and the rest of the squad squealed, delighted at the fanfare and just plain glad to be done. Glued together in a group hug, the mass of girls moved from the center of the stage toward the small set of steps that would take them back down to the floor and to their coach and fans.

Mina's heart beat eighty miles an hour. The thunderous chant, *Go Big Blue! Go Big Blue!* was dulled by the whoosh of blood in her ears, from her racing heart. She barely felt her feet touch the steps as she was carried by the flow of the squad, in between Kim and Sara.

"Oh my God, Mina," Kim exclaimed in one ear. "You totally nailed it, girl! Totally nailed it!"

Sara joined in excitedly, "I could feel your legs shaking before we popped you."

Mina nodded. Her legs were still rubbery. She still couldn't believe it was over. Just like that, two minutes and thirty seconds gone after months and months of grueling preparation. After the ugly, unproductive practice of the day before—one and done.

A nagging sense of event letdown reared its head. Sometimes it just seemed unfair that it was over so fast, but it didn't have time to sink in. Coach Embry waited for the girls at the landing.

Oh my God, is that a smile on her face? Mina wondered, in a daze.

Even when they'd nailed Counties, Coach Em refused to relax until after the winners were announced. But this time her usually serious face beamed back at the girls.

"Ladies, you looked awesome up there." She patted an arm or the back of any girl she was able to touch as they crowded around her. "I'm so proud of you."

Still breathing hard and heavy, the girls accepted the accolades. They clung to one another, adrenaline coursing through their veins from the quick, intense workout.

Coach Em signaled them to huddle closer and they obeyed.

"I know you want to visit your parents or . . ." she rolled her eyes. "Boyfriends."

Coach Em had a theory about boyfriends—they were a distraction and she wanted them as far away from cheer practice as possible. She even went so far as to black out their practices by taping thick construction paper in the small windows of the gym to keep peepers away.

But there was no venom in Coach's voice, just playful resignation. She could no more ban the girls from boy gazing and boy talk than she could will them to take first place. She went on, lowering her voice as the MC announced the next team, then raising it again as the music blared suddenly. "Make sure that everyone is back at the seats near the stage before the very last team performs."

She made her serious "I mean it" eyes at the girls. They nodded obediently. A few more ground rules followed—no unzipping their mock necks (Coach hated that even though the things were suffocating and hella hot), good sportsmanship toward other teams as they walked around (Embryism #20 "Saying 'good luck' or 'good job' never killed anybody"), and a half dozen other do's and don'ts.

Sara danced from one foot to the other beside Mina. She cocked her elbow onto Mina's shoulder before quickly letting it dangle at her side again.

Mina poked her side and they giggle-whispered.

Mina knew how Sara felt. She was just as restless. Her eyes gazed to the rear of the arena where the clique would be waiting for her, then to the area where her parents sat—at least where they had been two minutes before. Early on, her mother had told her that as soon as the Blue Devils went off, she and Mina's dad were heading for the lounge, a bar in the arena that stayed crowded with parents. Their empty seats shone amid the other seated Blue Devil fans.

There were so many people in there, as long as Lizzie, Kelly and Jacinta kept to the darkened corners of the arena, no way her parents would bump into them.

They should be good, she thought, before Coach Em's voice smacked her back into the lecture.

"Did you hear me, Mina?"

Mina blinked hard. "Sorry. I was looking for my parents."

Coach Em nodded. "Okay, okay. You guys can go. Be back before . . ."

She paused, expecting them to repeat the right answer.

"Before the last team performs," the girls chorused out of sync.

Coach Em walked away, off to join some of her coaching friends, and the girls dispersed into small cliques to discuss plans.

"I'm going to hang out with Chuck," Kim said. She turned to Mina and Sara. "Where are you guys going?"

"To find Brian and JZ," Mina said.

"I'm gonna hang with Mina," Sara said.

"We might try and find you guys."

"We'll be in the Blue Devils section of the bleachers," Mina hollered to Kim's retreating back.

She and Sara worked their way through the dense crowd.

"Well, we were awesome," Sara crowed. Still high from the performance, she speed-talked. "I still can't believe Lizzie, Jacinta and

Kelly came down here with JZ and Brian." She snorted. "So far so good hiding them from your parents, huh?"

"Yeah, but it's been a trip, though," Mina said.

"I bet," Sara laughed. "I won't be a fifth wheel, will I?"

Mina frowned. "No. It's just like last night at the condo, we're all just hanging out. It's not a couples' thing."

"Well you and Brian were totally coupled up, last night when we got back from the store."

"Yeah, but my parents weren't lurking nearby."

She and Sara were out of breath from pushing through the sea of bodies when they finally reached the clique in the easily identifiable Blue Devils section, swimming in blue and gold.

Jacinta, Kelly and Lizzie sat on the floor of the bottom bleacher, the safety rail partially obstructing their view of the stage and their legs dangling over the edge. The guys stood on the floor in front of the section. They clapped and yelled Mina and Sara's names as the girls walked up.

A minor stir rose as the rest of the section hooted too, before going back to their conversations. Just like that, no one was watching the stage anymore. Their team was done. Moving on.

"Y'all tore that joint up," JZ exclaimed.

Todd held out his program and a pen. "Can I have your autograph?"

Sara pretended to write her name as Todd faked a girlish giggle.

"Thanks y'all," Mina said. She buried her face in Brian's neck as he gave her a big hug and twirled her around.

"My girl was doing it big," Brian said. "Thought you were gonna flake out on that twist, though. I can't lie."

"Shoot, me too," Mina admitted as the clique laughed along in agreement. She adjusted her skirt and top once Brian put her down. Ignoring the stairs to their left, she and Sara boosted themselves over the rail and squeezed in between the girls.

"Alright, brother is hungry," JZ announced. "Who's trying head to the food court?"

Jacinta stood up. "I'll go."

Mina smacked her leg. "No you *won't*."

"Girl, why you rummin'?" JZ scowled.

Mina sucked her teeth. "Because my parents are out there right now." She gave Cinny a stern look. "Or have you forgotten you're a stowaway on this trip?"

"I forgot. I'm on lockdown, Jay," Jacinta said. She sat down reluctantly with a tiny thud.

"I'll go with you, dude," Todd said. He grabbed Lizzie's ankle and tugged playfully. "Want anything?"

"Diet Coke, please," she said shyly.

Jacinta snorted. "Diet? Whatever. JZ, can you get me some fries and a Sprite . . ." JZ nodded as Jacinta continued, "And a Twix."

"See, you need to be going yourself if you want all that," JZ said. He scrunched his eyebrows and pretended to count his change. "I thought you were gonna be a cheap date."

"Dag, how much cheaper can I be than a fries, soda and a candy bar?" Jacinta said, hands on her hips.

Mina shook her head as Brian looked over to see if she wanted anything.

As soon as the guys took off, Mina pumped the girls for every detail about life at the condo. She wouldn't let them leave out a single utterance, movement or thought.

"Dish," she commanded. "Where did you guys end up sleeping last night?"

Jacinta leaned up and spoke loud so Sara could hear. "Brian let us have the master bedroom."

"Aww, my Boo-Boo is so sweet," Mina said.

Sara made eyes at Lizzie. "No hook-ups?"

Lizzie's cheeks went an immediate crimson. "Uhh, no!"

"If you guys pull this off, you're the new queens," Sara said, awestruck.

"Queens of deceit," Kelly deadpanned.

"No," Sara said, "just the queens of ballsiness."

"For real," Mina nodded.

"I called my father last night and he seemed to believe we were at Aunt Jacqi's," Jacinta said.

Kelly laughed. "Unless he heard JZ yell in the background."

Lizzie winced. "Do you think he heard that, Cinny?"

"Why was JZ yelling?" Mina asked, completely caught up.

"Brian dropped a can of corn on his toe."

Jacinta, Lizzie and Kelly cracked up, thinking back on it.

Mina laughed too. But without the visual to back it up, her laugh was hollow. She could almost see JZ, howling and grabbing his toe—maybe cursing Brian out. But it was the type of thing where you had to be there to laugh as hard as the other girls were.

She soaked in every bittersweet word of the girls' adventure. Finally her best friend and her new friends were really friends on their own—had a little adventure to share that Mina could only look at from the outside. She peeked at Lizzie's face. It was animated with tense excitement. Mina smiled, pleased.

She dug for further details, relishing being brought up to speed. "Okay, why did Brian have a can of corn?"

Jacinta was laughing so hard, Kelly finished for her. "Who knows? But the three of us had gone into the bedroom so Cinny could call her dad and . . ."

"I knew it was going too well," Lizzie cut in. "She'd been talking to him for like . . ." She looked over at Kelly for confirmation.

"About ten minutes."

"No, it was longer than that," Jacinta said, her laughter now a hitched giggle. "It was like twenty."

"Right when she started in on the goodbye, this loud crash came from the kitchen," Kelly said. "I have never run to shut a door so fast in my life."

"And JZ screamed sooo loud," Lizzie said. "But Kelly had shut the door by then."

"He started cussing and we could still hear him," Jacinta laughed. "But you know how cellies are. I don't really think my father could hear the background noise."

"God, I hope not," Lizzie groaned.

The girls shared more of their night and morning at the condo until the guys came back, their arms full of goodies. As each boy went up to his respective girl, there was a minute of uncomfortable silence as Kelly and Sara sat, boyless.

Sara stood up. "Kelly, wanna go to the bathroom with me?"

Mina looked at Lizzie and Todd exchanging tickles and JZ and Jacinta laughing over something, then announced, "Wait, don't go. Hey y'all, I promised Sara no couple stuff."

"Oh, it's not that. I really have to go," Sara said.

"I'll go," Kelly said. She stood up, brushing off her pants daintily.

"Alright, you guys have . . ." Sara looked down at an imaginary watch on her wrist. "Five minutes and then no more kissy-kissy."

"You must be talking to them," Jacinta said, pointing her thumbs to either side of her to Mina and Lizzie.

"I'm talking to whoever," Sara laughed as she and Kelly climbed over the rail. "Five minutes. Starting now."

With them gone, Mina and Brian fell into a whispered conversation about nothing. He teased her about being able to see her legs shake from the jumbo screen, giving him an excuse to rub her calves suggestively.

JZ hoisted his tall frame over the rail and sat on the bleacher directly behind the girls.

"Man, I need sit down," he said to no one in particular.

He sat right behind Jacinta and began plucking with her, toeing her butt and throwing M&Ms into her hair.

She made a feeble attempt at fussing at him to stop. But the scowl never reached her smiling eyes.

"So how many more squads?" Brian asked.

Mina grabbed a stray program nearby. She ran her finger down the page, looked up at the screen to check which team was on the stage, then zoomed back down the page. "About ten," she announced.

"Ten?" JZ said. "We gotta stay for all of 'em?"

Mina leaned back and gave him a look.

"Man," he muttered under his breath. "I need a power bar or something to keep me awake."

"Hey . . . speaking of power bars, where's my candy?" Jacinta asked. She stood up. Her petite body stood guard in front of JZ. "Where's my Twix, Jay?"

He smiled. "I forgot it."

"For real?" She frowned.

"Look in his pocket, Cinny," Todd said.

"Todd," Lizzie scolded.

"Man!" JZ sucked his teeth.

Todd laughed. "My bad."

Jacinta held out her hand.

"Nope. I need it to keep my energy up through these next twenty hours," JZ said, rolling his eyes Mina's way.

"Exaggerate much?" Mina shot back.

"Okay, fifteen hours," Brian said.

"Okay, I'll remember this come summer league time," Mina said, addressing Brian, JZ and Todd. "When y'all want us sitting through five million games a night."

"Just jokes, girl," Brian said. He reached through the rail and chucked her chin, cutting her lecture short. He moved his face closer to hers and she pecked his lips with a shy kiss.

"Come on, Jay. I'm really in the mood for one," Jacinta pleaded.

JZ took the candy bar from his jacket pocket and slowly unpeeled the wrapper.

"Aww see, you so wrong," Jacinta said. She swiped at the bar, missing. JZ jerked it skyward, high above his head. Jacinta lunged, but still couldn't get a grip.

The couples laughed as Jacinta dropped onto JZ's lap, tugging at his arm.

"Oh yeah. Give him a lap dance, Cinny," Todd cat-called.

He and Brian knocked fists.

Jacinta stood on the bleacher, straddling JZ's lap, so she was nearly as tall as his arms were high. Finally, stretching her body as long as it would go, she plucked the golden wrapped bar out of his hands, before sitting back down on his lap, legs crossed primly, satisfied.

"You owe me seventy-five cents, girl," he groused good-naturedly.

Jacinta took a big chunk from one of the Twix bars, munching contentedly. She crunched near JZ's ear and he palmed her face.

As she laughed, Twix cookie crumbs blew in his face.

"Now who's wrong?" JZ asked, eyebrow cocked high.

But Mina noticed he didn't make Jacinta get up. She shook her head at their little show then looked toward the bathroom, checking for signs of Sara and Kelly. The couples' five minutes of canoodling was way up.

Her eyes froze on a figure steamrolling their way.

"Cinny," Mina called out in a strained, strangled yell-whisper.

Jacinta pulled out the other half of the Twix bar and put it in front of JZ's mouth. He took a tiny nibble.

"Cinny," Mina yell-whispered again, more insistent.

Jacinta looked down at her. "What?"

Mina nodded to her right, in the direction of the arena's main doors.

Jacinta squinted at her. "What?" She parroted Mina's loud whisper.

"Raheem," Mina yell-whispered.

"What? What about Rah . . ." Jacinta frowned. She finally looked in the direction Mina's eyes refused to leave. In a flash she caught an eyeful of Raheem running their way, his face twisted into the nastiest snarl she'd ever seen.

Meltdown in . . . 1

"If I could escape, I would."
—Gwen Stefani, "Sweet Escape"

Some old school phrases have absolutely no meaning in real life. They lost any real definition ages ago. But as Raheem zigzagged his way through the crowd, his angry eyes blazing and his normally neatly braided hair out in a wild jagged afro, one of Mina's grandmother's favorite phrases not only came to mind, but made perfect sense. Unable to take her eyes off his face, Mina knew in her bones that things were about to "go to hell in a handbasket."

She had no friggin' idea what a handbasket was. But it didn't stop her from knowing that right now she was inside of one and it was sliding fast into a bad place.

Thank God I'm not in it alone, was her last thought when Raheem finally made it to the bleachers.

Jacinta popped off JZ's lap so fast, Mina wasn't sure if JZ hadn't helped her with a shove. His face was confused and knowing all at once, but he stayed seated on the bleacher and surprised Mina by leaning back. His elbows rested casually on the empty row behind them.

JZ's sudden casual stance made Mina's stomach clench. No way JZ felt that at ease. But seeing him act like it, sent off every alarm in Mina's head. Without knowing it, she gripped Brian's forearm and barely felt him loosen her fingers. He held her two fingers lightly and turned his body toward Raheem, positioning himself to see better.

"Jacinta what the fu . . ." Raheem started before Jacinta cut him off.

"What are you doing here?" A tiny tremor underneath the nonchalant question made her voice crack on the last word.

Raheem's eyes bucked in surprise. "You sitting on some other dude's lap and all you gon' ask me is what *I'm* doing here?" He glanced over Jacinta's shoulder at JZ. "What *you* doing here?!"

Their raised voices didn't cause a stir. The music was so loud that everyone in the arena was screaming to be heard over the noise.

The blaring voice of the competition's MC reminded everyone to stop and get their spirit gear from the House of Cheer, at booth ten.

Angel, who had gotten lost in the crowd trying to keep up with Raheem, finally arrived at the bleachers. His chest heaving, he put his hand firmly on Raheem's shoulder and yell-whispered something in Spanish. Raheem took his voice down, but if anything, his anger went up two notches. He spat every word.

"So, what? This you now?" Raheem nodded curtly at JZ, who was somehow managing to look cool as a cuke.

Jacinta folded her arms tight across her chest. "No, Raheem." The heavy unuttered sigh in her voice said she was used to arguing over sillier stuff than this. "You know me and Jason just friends."

"What up, kid?" JZ finally said. He leaned up, resting his elbows on his thighs and stretched his fist through the safety rail for a pound, shrugged when Raheem ignored it, and sat back.

"Something must be up." Raheem wouldn't take his eyes off Jacinta. "Why you sneak all the way down here if ain't nothing up with you and dude?"

"Because my girl Mina performed tonight," Jacinta said. Her voice had gone from worried to weary. She walked over and down the side steps and joined Raheem on the floor. She addressed Angel this time. "So, what's up, Angel? What are y'all doing here?"

"Chilling, mami," Angel said. His eyes locked on Jacinta's for a second, sending a silent message no one but Cinny understood.

Jacinta's head took a barely visible dip as she nodded.

Just then Kelly and Sara came back, stopping right beside Angel and Jacinta.

Sara looked around at the newcomers, confused, waiting for an introduction that would never come.

But Kelly's face was a clear "uh-oh." Mina saw it.

Uh-oh is right, she thought.

"Angel, I . . . what are you guys doing here?" Kelly said.

Jacinta glanced over at Kelly. "Yeah, Kelly, what *are* they doing here?"

"I . . . Angel said . . ." Kelly kept her eyes on Angel as she finished. "Angel mentioned they might come but I didn't . . . you know, I thought you were joking."

"Yeah, 'cause if he wasn't joking you would have told me, right?" Jacinta's eyebrows dipped into a deep furrow.

Mina couldn't keep up with the telepathic messages being sent. But it didn't take a psychic to know that a lot of stuff was being unsaid.

"Yeah, she probably would have gave you a heads-up so you could kept your little dirt on the low," Raheem said.

"I don't have nothing to keep on the low," Jacinta snapped. "Me and Jay just friends. And you know what? Me and you just friends too. So why you bringing beef?"

"Look, I'm not gon' sit here and have my business all out there." Raheem grabbed her arm and began pulling her away. His grip bit into her flesh.

Jacinta tried pushing his hand off. "Stop, Raheem."

"Man, come on," Angel said, soft but firm. "Don't do this. Not here."

JZ stood up and came to the top of the small stairway. Brian instinctively stood up straighter, ready to have JZ's back. Todd's body language remained neutral, but he stood his ground next to Brian.

Mina's stomach pitched and dove into her bladder as Brian's hand fell away from hers. *I should have gone to the bathroom with Kelly and Sara,* she thought stupidly.

"Man, look, Cinny's telling the truth," JZ said. "I got mad respect for you. I wouldn't be tipping with your girl. We was just rummin'."

For the first time, Raheem took his eyes off Jacinta, really took them away from her and looked JZ up and down. They fought hard on the court and field when Sam-Well played Del Rio Bay High—but they also played together during summer league and when JZ went to The Cove for a pick-up game. They weren't friends, but respectful opponents.

Raheem's eyes narrowed and it was like a fire going out. Mina felt the tension fade for just a second.

Raheem let go of Jacinta's arm and walked over to JZ, his hand extended for a pound.

"Alright, kid, I take your word for it," he said. They exchanged a pound. "I don't have no beef with you. Real talk."

He turned back to Jacinta, his voice eerily casual and out of place when paired with his wild hair. "Look, let me holler at you for a second. Alright?"

Jacinta shook her head, but turned toward the door in compliance. Before following him, she looked up at Mina. "I'll be back."

"Kelly, what is going on?" Mina asked. She ducked her head under the rail and slid down to the floor. "Why is Angel here?"

They all clustered around Kelly. She tucked at her hair and looked over at Angel for help. He was watching Jacinta and Raheem walk over to a dark corner at the end of the bleachers near the main door, his jaw tight.

"Angel, I really thought you were joking about coming down," Kelly said.

"I wanted to see you and you know I wasn't gon' leave my boy home," Angel said. "Why you ain't tell me that Cinny was hooking up with kid?"

"I already said it's not like that," JZ said gruffly.

"Like what?" Kelly asked, confused.

"Cinny was sitting on JZ's lap when Raheem came in," Lizzie explained.

Kelly's face went "oh" again as the realization hit her. "Why didn't you text me to tell me you were coming?" Kelly asked.

Angel picked up the accusation in her voice and shot back, "I was trying to surprise you. I didn't think no stupid shit was gonna jump off."

"I think we should make sure Cinny is alright," Mina said, gazing in the direction the two had gone.

"Mina, we need to get back to the squad soon," Sara said. "It's only like three more teams left."

"Heem ain't gonna do nothing stupid," Angel said. But he wasn't too convinced because he looked up quickly to the corner to check on things. Assured it was still cool he reassured them, "He just want talk to her."

"He's pissed," Todd said.

Mina rolled her eyes. "Gee, you think?"

Todd threw his hands up, as if Mina were about to strike him. "Woah, don't get mad at me."

"T, I'm sorry. I just think we should be closer, in case . . ." Mina stopped herself from outright accusing Raheem of anything.

She looked to Brian, but knew what he was going to say before he said it in a calm, reasonable voice. "That's their business."

"But she's our friend," Lizzie said.

Lizzie's backup put Mina into action. "Come on . . . we'll just stand off to the side."

The girls, with Sara reluctantly following—one eye on the stage—headed to the darkened corner where Raheem's long-sleeved white tee beckoned like a signal. They could see his arms gesturing and as they got closer could see his face, angrier than before, looking down at Jacinta, shaking as he fussed.

They stood close in a classic lover's-quarrel stance.

Jacinta's arms were still folded, her head cocked upward, looking into Raheem's tight-jawed face.

Mina was glad to see Jacinta didn't seem nervous anymore.

Just as the girls got to the corner of the bleachers, leaving about ten feet between them and the couple, Raheem's arm came up and smacked Jacinta in the face. There was a collective gasp from the group and everyone but Mina froze.

She ran over to Jacinta, her body shaking from fear and anger. "What is wrong with you?" she hollered into his face before turning to Jacinta. "Are you okay, Cinny?"

Jacinta nodded. Tears brimmed in her eyes. Miraculously they pooled in her eyes for the longest time before ever spilling.

When Mina turned back to Raheem the rest of the clique was there beside her, even the guys, who had obviously seen the slap too.

"You guys aren't even a couple anymore," Mina fussed. "Just leave her alone."

"This not your business, Mina," Raheem warned. His eyes were mean slits. "Cinny always said you were nosy. But this time you need step."

"Yeah, I'll step, but I'm taking Cinny with me," Mina said, her voice shaky. She grabbed Jacinta's hand and turned.

Raheem grabbed Jacinta's other arm. "I didn't mean to hit you, Cinny. You got me all . . ."

Jacinta reared her hand back and smacked him in the face. "Don't you ever hit me again."

She let herself be led off by Mina.

Raheem snatched away as Angel pulled his arm.

"Man, look, let's just . . ." Angel head-checked, making sure security or any other adults weren't about to intervene. But the music was loud, the crowd was thick and no one seemed to even know their drama was unfolding. He wanted to keep it that way. He elbowed Raheem, lightly, in the back. "Walk outside with me for a hot minute, son."

Raheem backed away, never taking his eyes off the girls huddled around Jacinta.

"Cinny, look . . . let me holler for a minute. Come outside with me and Angel," he called, his eyes more hurt than angry now as he pleaded. "Just for a minute, damn."

Jacinta never looked up.

Brian, JZ and Todd stood off to the side of the huddle, their faces tight, ready to protect the girls if it came to that. But Raheem and Angel walked off, quickly lost in the mass of people as they neared the doors.

"He's a real jerk," Sara said.

Mina shook her head at Sara. Sara didn't know, of course, but even if Raheem was acting like a complete ass tonight, this wasn't the end of their chapter, more like the beginning of another one. That's one thing Mina had learned over the last few months. She didn't completely understand it. But she knew one thing, calling Raheem names wasn't going to help anything.

Sara got the message and nodded. Apologetically, she reminded Mina, "Ummm . . . Mi, we've got to get back."

"Cinny, I'm sorry but me and Sara have to go."

Jacinta wiped her eyes quickly and sniffed. "Naw, it's cool. I didn't mean to ruin y'all competition."

"Girl, please," Mina said, not knowing what else to say. "Tonight at the beach party we'll make Raheem voodoo dolls and stick pins in them."

Jacinta chuckled as she wiped a few stray tears and the girls giggled nervously.

Just then, a voice they all recognized killed the laughter immediately.

"Cinny? Lizzie? Kelly? What are you girls doing here?"

"Shit, Mi, it's your moms," JZ whispered, as if the girls didn't know that.

And the Winner Is . . .

"I am number one. No matter if you like it."
—Nelly, "Number One"

Mina felt like she was underwater. Everything around her was happening slower. Even the cacophony of music, people cheering, talking, laughing and screaming seemed dulled. Since her mother had unceremoniously sent her and Sara back to the front of the arena with a simple, teeth-clenched "Go sit with your squad, girls," Mina had been hopelessly trying to tread to the surface.

She risked a glance back and to her right, where her parents sat in the second row. Lizzie, Jacinta and Kelly now shared the two seats her parents had occupied, while Jackson and Mariah Mooney stood guard at the end of the row. Mariah's eyes bore laser beams in the girls' general direction as she spoke to her husband, no doubt bringing him up to speed. Jackson Mooney nodded along, his brown face looking weary.

Mina's shoulders sagged. She didn't have to know what her mom was saying to know it was all bad. She and Sara had been sent away before her mom broke into a lecture, but as they walked off Mina could hear Mariah going totally parental on each and every one of her friends.

Sara gave Mina's knee a reassuring pat. But her eyes drooped with sadness that said both "I feel for you," and "Better you than me."

Around them the squad buzzed excitedly.

The final squad ended their performance and the house lights went up, washing the arena in bright, fluorescent lighting. The DJ, on cue, switched to line-dance music and the obedient mob of cheerleaders rushed the open floor in front of the stage and began the cha-cha slide.

Kim pulled at Mina. "Let's go try our new moves."

Mina reluctantly followed along. Her squad mates giggled and bumbled their way through a version of the dance they'd made up just last night. Every squad added their own touch to the line dances and the Blue Devil squad had chosen an ambitious drop-it-like-it's-hot squat and turn, in place of the usual step.

"Mina, if you guys are gonna get in trouble, you worrying won't change that," Sara said in her ear as they cha-cha'd to the right. "May as well have some fun."

Sara linked arms with her and they cha-cha'd left before doing the squat and falling on their butts. Laughing maniacally, they scrambled up to avoid being trampled by the squad.

"Just consider it like your last meal before the sentencing," Sara chuckled dryly.

Mina groaned. Sara's description was way closer than she knew.

After two more line dances and a random free-style to "Cotton-Eyed Joe," the MC popped from behind the curtain and teased the crowd, asking if they were ready to hear the winners. Despite the crowd's roar, it wasn't enough. The MC pretended to step back off-stage until the noise was deafening.

The Blue Devil squad sat on the floor, cross-legged, knee-to-knee, holding hands. Sara and Kim had a death grip on Mina's hands. The slight pain forced her attention away from the MC's rambling about winners of the Jump and Tumble event.

She'd worked hard to get here. Sara was right, she needed to savor this moment. Later would be another story.

As the MC moved closer and closer to her team's division, Mina felt the adrenaline kick in again. Her blood seemed to sprint through her veins as she hoped against hope to hear their names called for the top spot.

"Ladies," Coach Em's voice came from beside them. "Good sportsmanship, remember?"

The girls nodded absently, focused on the stage.

"And in the medium Varsity division . . ." the MC said.

It was Mina's turn to squeeze hands as she prayed their names would be nowhere near the honorable mention spots. She gripped Kim and Sara's hands until the announcement of the four hon men spots, places eight through five, were finished.

Kim squeezed back insanely hard until the fourth place was mentioned.

They smiled at one another when their name wasn't called.

Third would be respectable based on the tough competition, Mina told herself. But she wasn't kidding anyone. They'd already beaten out five teams. She didn't want third.

"God, please, please not third," Sara chanted under her breath, echoing Mina's sentiments.

"And in third, those sassy ladies . . ." The MC, an obvious expert in torture, held the answer to herself just a beat before announcing gleefully, "The Oliver Whelan Wahoos!"

Mina and Sara both let out a huge breath, then laughed at their twin reactions. They shushed themselves before Coach Em caught wind of their celebration. It was unsportsmanlike to celebrate avoiding being placed lower in the ranks.

"We might do this, guys. We might take first," Kim whispered, awestruck by the possibility.

Mina couldn't stand it anymore. Her hands gripped tight with her squad mates', she took a deep breath and lowered her head, hoping they'd dodge one last bullet and avoid being called second.

It didn't matter that second for them would be a huge victory.

When you've come this far, you can't help it—you want first, Mina thought.

"Alright," the MC said, frustratingly teasing. "Who's our second place winners? Who do you guys think?"

The crowd's answers were unintelligible. The MC smiled anyway, as if they'd just shared a secret with her. "Well, let's see." She peeked down at the five-by-six index card in her hand. "In second place . . . the feisty Blue Devils of Del Rio Bay High!"

Instant emotions of joy and slight disappointment slammed Mina's head up. She was pulled standing by the force of the squad. They jumped up squealing and hugging.

Kim and Sara had her in a bear hug. They all jumped up and down in sync until Renee, the co-captain, pulled Kim away. They ran up to the stage to collect the huge silver trophy.

Coach Em hugged the huddle. She praised the girls, openly relieved and clearly ecstatic with second.

"Oh my God we did it!" Sara yelled, embracing Mina tight.

"I can't believe it. We beat six teams," Mina said, dazed.

"And three of them are Extreme vets," Joss said.

"And there was no way we could have beat the Hornets," Cassidy said. "They were the grand champs last year."

"Oh my God, we almost beat the grand champs," Joss squealed, sending off a new round of hugs and jumping.

During their celebration the girls missed the Hornets being called first. Coach Em would probably reprimand them a bit about that later. It was disrespectful to celebrate so long. But it felt so good.

The girls flocked to the trophy, like bees to honey, when Kim and Renee returned.

Soon they were surrounded by parents taking photos of them beside it, cheesing.

Somehow Coach Em shooed them away from their floor spot and back toward the walls, far away from the stage where the Large division announcements rang out. The picture-taking and mugging went on for another ten minutes.

Parents and classmates hugged, congratulated the girls and squeezed into a couple photos with the four-foot-tall trophy.

Every now and then Mina randomly hugged a squad mate. Funny how seconds ago she'd hoped against second place. Now, she and everyone else were already bragging. After all, six other teams were going away with nothing more than a memory and a certificate. They were second place National champs.

"So we'll catch up at the beach later, right?" Kim said.

The question shoved Mina back into the present.

Before she could answer, her parents, with Lizzie, Kelly and Jacinta in tow, were in front of her. It was like the question had brought them there.

The anger in their eyes from earlier was replaced with smiles.

Mina squeezed in, cheesing, as her mom waved some of the girls standing by in for a photo with the trophy.

"We're so proud of you, boo," her mom said.

Jackson hugged Mina tight. "Good job, baby girl."

"Tonight, okay," Kim whispered before being pulled off into another photo.

Mina nodded.

Tonight.

Right.

Are You Stupid or Just Dumb?

"What don't kill me, makes me stronger than be-fo'."
—Jay-Z, "American Gangster"

Once Jackson Mooney had gotten them out of the arena's snarled parking lot, it was smooth sailing. He rolled his Navigator along O.C.'s four-lane strip. The car was dead silent. He looked into his rearview mirror at the pensive girls in the backseat.

Mina and Lizzie sat in the second row, faces somber. Lizzie's was pale except for two splotches of color on her cheeks. Mina met his gaze then quickly looked straight ahead.

Jacinta and Kelly were in the third seat, shadows to him from the front.

There was more than enough room for three girls to sit in the second row, but they were taking the safety in numbers approach, coupling off for support.

Smart girls, he thought.

They were going to need one another's support. His wife was on fire tonight. She broke his thoughts, her clipped voice penetrating the silent car.

"Let me ask you girls something," Mariah said. She flipped open her passenger-side mirror and gazed into it, making eye contact with Mina and Lizzie. "Are you stupid or just dumb?"

She paused. But the girls weren't that stupid. They knew it was a rhetorical question. Mariah proved them right by jumping feet-first into her lecture. Her eyes blazed. "What in the world was going through your minds to come all the way down here with the boys like that?"

She looked directly at Lizzie, this time expecting an answer.

The splotches on Lizzie's face went from dull crimson to bright red. She cleared her throat. "We . . ." She turned, hoping Jacinta would jump in. But Jacinta remained, smartly, quiet. "We didn't feel like sitting home," Lizzie finished lamely.

Mariah's voice was shrill. "And so you drove two hours away from home with not one single adult knowing where you were going?" She shook her head. "What if something had happened to you? Where in the world do Marybeth and Patrick think you are, Lizzie?"

"At Cinny's," Lizzie whispered.

Mariah turned in her seat and looked at what she knew was Jacinta's shadow. "And where does Jacqi think you are?"

"Home," Jacinta said, equally meek.

"Home?" Jackson asked, confused. "How can she think you're home?"

"She's in New York," Jacinta said.

Mariah threw her hands in the air. When they came down and smacked her thighs, Mina flinched. "What? She's not even home? Does your father know?"

Jacinta shook her head, then, realizing Mrs. Mooney couldn't see that, said quietly, "No. I mean he knows Aunt Jacqi is gone . . . but . . ."

"Kelly, I suppose your grandmother also thinks you're over at Jacinta's?" Mariah's voice was weary. Her head tick tocked back and forth, incredulous, with each new detail.

"Yes . . . yes, ma'am," Kelly said.

"I would ask you girls what you would have done if there had been a car accident, but I know you have no idea how to answer," Jackson said. "It's obvious you weren't thinking at all to pull a stunt like this."

"Mina, did you know they were going to do this?" Mariah asked, her voice sharp.

Mina wanted to lie so badly.

Lizzie reached for her hand and squeezed softly.

Save yourself, the squeeze said. *Just say no.*

But Mina couldn't lie.

"Yes," she said softly. "I found out yesterday. They were at Individuals last night."

"Did you know they were *planning* this?" Jackson asked. He took his eyes off the road long enough to watch for Mina's response.

Relief was in her eyes as she answered no.

She didn't know why she felt relief. The hole was dug and it was mad deep. Still, the fact that she wasn't a part of the original planning was the only pro in a long list of cons and she held on to it for dear life.

There was sweet relief from the inquisition as Jackson pulled the car into the hotel parking garage. The girls filed out of the truck, silently. The truck doors echoed loudly in the empty garage. They were among the first people back from the competition, adding to the desolation closing in around the girls.

No one spoke a word as they rode the elevator to the fifth floor room.

The girls walked the hall, littered with blue and gold streamers, posters and other Blue Devil paraphernalia, reminded of the fun they'd be missing out on.

Her father stuck his plastic key into the door's lock. The light click of the lock, the sound of the girls' freedom dissolving, roared in Mina's ears.

They filed into the room and bunched into a corner, unsure what to do.

"Sit down, girls," Mariah directed.

They sat, hip-to-hip, on the double bed.

Mina's mom stood in front of them. Her face was tight, but the anger in her eyes had subsided. Mina's dad took a seat on the dresser, happy to let his wife do the talking.

"There are a million reasons why what you girls did was dumb as dirt," Mariah said, then sighed. "Lizzie, I'm especially surprised that you'd pull something like this."

Tears streamed down Lizzie's face. Mina put her arm around her.

Jackson chuckled. "Are those tears because you got caught?"

Lizzie sniffled. "Yes."

An involuntary nervous giggle escaped Mina's throat. Lizzie was too honest for her own good.

"I'm going to call your parents and let them know you're here, safe with me," Mariah said.

"Can't you just call them tomorrow?" Lizzie begged.

Mariah rolled her eyes and gave Lizzie a "what do you think" smirk.

"How girls who are usually very bright and responsible get themselves into this kind of mess is beyond me," Mariah said. She folded her arms and took inventory of the small huddle on the bed. "Anyone care to enlighten me?"

"We're sorry," Jacinta said.

"For getting caught," Jackson quipped. The whole thing now seemed to amuse him.

"If we had asked for permission to ride down with JZ and stay with you guys, our parents would have said no," Lizzie said.

Mariah frowned. "How do you know that, Lizzie?"

Lizzie's mouth moved wordlessly.

"Exactly. You don't know that," Mariah said. "If you had asked, you know your mom would have called me. We would have debated how safe it was to drive with Brian and then made a decision. And you know what? I think she would have let you."

Lizzie slumped against Mina.

"Well, I have some calls to make." Mariah walked out of the room with her cell phone in hand and Jackson followed.

"Could we be in any more trouble?" Lizzie asked miserably.

"What did my mom say after me and Sara left?" Mina whispered.

"She looked around and asked where was Michael," Kelly said.

"Yeah, and when we told her he was home she said he had more sense than all of us put together," Lizzie said.

She and Mina exchanged a knowing nod and eye roll. It wasn't that Michael was any more sensible. He'd done his fair share of crazy things with the clique. Heck, he was even the best liar of the four of them. But you couldn't tell Mariah that. She always called Michael the responsible one.

"She went off when she found out that we'd stayed at Brian's condo last night," Jacinta said.

Mina's heart skipped a beat. She had forgotten about that tidbit.

"Why didn't you guys lie and say you just came down today?" Mina asked.

"Phhh, okay, lie," Jacinta said. "We were already caught wrong. Besides, didn't your mother know the guys were coming on Friday?"

Mina nodded.

Jacinta eyebrows raised as if to say, "well then."

They hushed when the door opened. Mariah motioned for Lizzie.

Lizzie stood, composed herself and walked over to the phone Mariah held out.

She and Mariah walked out to the hallway for privacy and the girls only caught Lizzie's voice as it began to quiver an apology.

When Lizzie returned, Mariah was already on the phone with Jacinta's father. "Hi Jamal, it's Mariah Mooney," she said, as she stood in front of the girls. "Yeah, it's pretty nice down here. Nearly seventy-five, earlier." The steely look she leveled at the girls clashed with the light laugh in her voice. "Well, look, I wish I was calling just to tell you the squad won." She laughed again. "But, these girls of ours have been busy scheming. Jacinta is down here with me." She paused as Mr. Phillips reacted, then nodded along. "Nobody was more surprised than me to see them at the arena, Jamal. Un-huh. But look, they're going to stay with me tonight." She paused again, scowled. "Oh no, don't do that. Don't come all the way down here." She snapped her fingers at Jacinta, signaling her to come get the phone. "No, it's not a problem at all. I'll bring her home tomorrow. Un-huh." She laughed. "Tell me about it. Okay, well look, here's Jacinta. Okay. No problem, Jamal."

She handed the phone over and pointed to the hallway, directing Jacinta out for privacy. By the time she'd called Mae Bell Lopez and explained once more it was no problem for the girls to stay with them for the night, an hour had passed.

The last call, to Kelly's grandmother, had ended right on time. The hallways were now full of chattering cheerleaders, families and slamming doors.

Now that the girls' secret had been shared with every parent, the tension in the room had dwindled to an uncomfortable uncertainty.

What now? Mina thought, growing antsy at the growing hallway noise.

Jackson Mooney answered without being asked. "Well, I'm not the one punished." He winked at the girls. "The Final Four is on tonight. I'm heading to the lounge to watch the game."

He kissed his wife on the cheek then opened his arms for a hug from Mina.

"You stuck your foot in it this time, baby girl," he whispered good-naturedly.

Mina nodded. A lump grew in her throat. Without her dad to play good cop, they were at the mercy of her mom.

"See you in a few hours," Jackson said, before slipping out the door.

The noise from the hall filtered through like a sliver of freedom, emboldening Mina.

"Mom, can we still go to the beach party tonight?" she asked, and almost flinched away from her mother's glare.

"No you didn't just ask me that."

"Mommy, please," Mina begged. She didn't care if she lost this battle. It had to be fought. She was fighting for her life . . . well, her social life. And right now they felt like the same thing. "We know we're in the world's worst pot of boiling water. But . . . I mean, don't you want to watch the game with Daddy?"

"Amina, have you lost your mind?" Mariah sat on the bed opposite the girls. Her brown eyes pierced each girl. "What you girls did was . . ."

"They just wanted to come support me," Mina said, joining her mom on the bed. "If we had left Thursday instead of Wednesday, they could have come."

Mariah scowled, cocking her head as if she'd misheard. "Are you saying this is me and Daddy's fault because we wanted to leave a day early?"

"No, I . . . I didn't mean that," Mina backpedaled. "I just . . . the only reason Lizzie couldn't come was because we left too early. It wasn't that Mr. and Mrs. O'Reilly were against her coming."

"Lord, that makes total sense in Mina land, doesn't it?" Mariah chuckled in spite of her annoyance. She shook her head, eyeing the girls who sat pensive, and ramrod straight on the edge of the other bed, then looked into Mina's hopeful eyes.

"They just wanted to show me some love, Ma," Mina pleaded. "Can't we go for a little while? The squad's expecting me."

"What if I let you go and not the girls?" Mariah smirked.

Mina blanched.

"Okay, I don't mean any harm y'all . . ." Mina twisted her mouth as she thought about it. "But . . . you're about to get left."

Mariah surprised them by laughing out loud. She smacked Mina's leg.

"See how your girl does you after you came all this way to see her?"

"Thanks a lot, Princess," Jacinta grumbled.

But the scent of hope was in the air for the first time since they'd been busted.

Pimp-slapped into Reality

"It ain't fresh, to just let him call the shots."
—Trey Songz, "Can't Help But Wait"

Mina stripped out of her cheer uniform and into a pair of capris, a long-sleeved spirit tee and her Blue Devil flops, in record time. She grabbed several cheer blankets, kissed her mother's cheek hastily and sped out, the girls barreling behind her.

It had taken twenty minutes and a *lot* of rules later, but they had broken Mina's mom down. Her final words still echoed in their ears: "You better enjoy tonight. Because life will be nothing short of lockdown the second we get back home."

Not one of them questioned the truth in her words.

They got off the elevator, stepped onto the hotel's outdoor patio and Mina shot Brian a text "–mt us on bch."

She inhaled a lungful of the sea air, wanting, needing to enjoy every second of the night. They had until 10:45 PM.

"And not a second later. Not one second, girls," her mom had warned.

The girls had to be in the room by 10:45. Not just leaving the beach, *in* the room.

Their legs slogged through the sand faster than it should have been possible as they made their way to the spot where a full party was already in progress.

More than one hundred people, some coupled off on beach

blankets or towels, most others standing in small clusters or large packs, made a wide messy circle around twenty kerosene lanterns— a substitute for a bonfire, which wasn't allowed.

The lanterns provided limited light. The partyers were shadowed figures, well outside the steady flickering. Cardboard boxes, stacked three high, served as the DJ booth where a pair of portable speakers, facing away from the crashing waves, was hooked to a music player. The song switched from pop rock to hip-hop and blared, bass-less, into the night. Every few seconds a whitish glow emitted from spots among the clusters, people dialing or checking their cell phones as one of the Extreme Moments pictures was texted around.

Mina ignored the buzzing of her phone. The pictures had been coming in steadily since last night. Her text bill was going to be in-sane.

The girls crept around the clusters. Mina peered into the dark-ness, stopping to peek her head into a cluster every few feet, to find Kim or Sara. The girls chatted a few minutes at each cluster before moving on. Congratulations went out to Mina each time they stopped.

Minutes later, she approached a group of six girls and five guys. Everyone had either a large red plastic cup or a bottle in their hand. As Mina got closer she recognized that all the girls were dressed the same—not identical, but close—in pastel colored polos and patch-work shorty shorts. There was only one group of girls hokey enough to dare dressing alike without risking open ridicule. Mina tried to veer off quickly but her feet got tangled, slowing her turn. It was too late.

"Hey, Mina," Jessica chirped.

"Umph, she is so phony," Jacinta whispered from behind Mina.

Mina didn't have time to debate the merit of Jess's sincerity, even though her instincts told her the Jess she'd encounter tonight would be nothing like the Jess from Wednesday night. But they were less than three feet away from the girl. She couldn't just act like she didn't see her.

Instead, she forced sun into her voice and asked, "Hey, Jess. Know where Sara is?"

Jessica waved the hand holding the red cup toward a vague and random area near the water. Mina took a step back as liquid sloshed over the side, nearly spilling on her.

"Over there somewhere."

"Big help," Jacinta muttered under her breath.

It was loud enough to hear, but Jessica ignored it. Since the sociology project, the two had made good on their joint promise to pretend the other didn't exist.

"Hey, it's Mina and her merry band of mid-pops," Mari-Beth said.

The rest of the Glams, on cue, laughed their high-pitched, well-practiced Stepford friends laugh.

Mari-Beth swished her thick blonde hair, then raked it to the left side so it draped perfectly on her shoulder. Her eyes narrowed and a sneer-smile spread across her face. "I hope you guys are staying for the big fireworks."

"Who's doing fireworks?" Lizzie asked. She absently scoured the beach.

"It's going to be awesome," Mari-Beth said, addressing only Mina. She cocked her head, as if thinking. "What time are they again, Jess?"

Jessica raked her weave with her fingers. "Another hour or so."

"Oh good. It'll be fun. Be sure to stick around for 'em, *Mina*," Mari-Beth ordered before turning her attention away from the girls, dismissing them.

Mina rolled her eyes, but was thankful for the curtain call. She and the girls moved in the direction Jessica had pointed.

"They make my skin crawl," Kelly said.

"I'm not sure what's creepier, Mi. Them hating you or . . ." Lizzie made air quotes. "Liking you." She shuddered and absently zipped her jacket to the neck.

Mina snorted. "Trust, I'm just as weirded out. But it's just until tomorrow. Monday we go back to hating, no quotes needed."

They ended their search, choosing instead to spread the cheer blankets and camp out among a bunch of others. All four of them plopped down on the largest blanket. Seconds later Mina's phone rang and she guided the guys to their spot.

Todd ran up to the blanket. He stood behind Mina, bent way over until his upside-down face was in hers, his blonde mop tickling her forehead.

"What are you doing?" she asked, palming his face and shoving it away.

He inspected each girl up close, first Kelly then Jacinta, turning their arms and hands over, finally ending at Lizzie. She squirmed as his finger slid down the collar of her polo while he examined her neck.

He threw his hands up in exaggerated bafflement. "Well you guys *look* okay."

"What's wrong with your boy, Liz?" Jacinta asked.

Todd plopped down next to Lizzie, shoulder-to-shoulder. "I was just checking to see if anyone was bruised or battered. The way Mina's mom was on the warpath I expected some casualties. Ya know, a shiner here." He patted his butt. "A sore butt there."

The girls exchanged knowing glances in the dark.

"Oh something got battered alright," Mina said with a snort.

Lizzie chimed in. "Yeah, our chances of ever seeing the light of day once we get back home."

The girls un-huh'd along as JZ and Brian settled down. Brian sat close behind Mina, his arms draped over his steepled knees.

"Shoot, I know that's right," JZ said. He sat down beside Jacinta, keeping a good friendly distance between them. "She mad laid into us when you and Sara left."

"Yeah, Cinny told me." Mina leaned back on Brian. "I don't even want to talk about it. This is probably my last night out for a lonnnng time. Let's pretend we won't be on punishment for life."

The girls nodded solemnly.

JZ wrapped his arms around his legs. He head-checked Jacinta's way as he asked, "So you alright?"

Jacinta uncrossed her legs then changed her mind and crossed them again. She cleared her throat, uncomfortable as six pairs of eyes glowed in her direction in the dark.

"I'm cool," she said quietly.

"Ay, I need to give some dap to Super Mi over there," JZ said. He leaned over, his fist out for a pound. "You rolled up on Raheem like you were ready to fight."

Mina tapped his fist lightly with hers. "Shoot, but I felt like running behind Cinny and hiding when he told me to mind my own business."

"Thanks for having my back, Mina," Jacinta mumbled.

Lizzie peered through the darkness at everyone's face. "So do you think they went back to Del Rio Bay?"

"Nope," Kelly said. She looked up from checking her Sidekick.

"You say that like you know," Jacinta said.

Kelly stood up. "I do. Angel just texted me. He and Raheem are in the front parking lot."

She looked down into everyone's questioning faces then focused in on Jacinta. "He asked me to come out there and to bring you."

"Just tell him she doesn't want to come," Mina snapped. Raheem had a lot of nerve. She started to say so when Jacinta stood up.

JZ snorted loud, clearly offended, and stood up abruptly. "Alright, I'm going see what's up in this joint." He gave Brian and Todd a pound. "Check me some fly shortaayyys."

He walked off before anyone could say another word.

"Cinny, you're going out there?" Mina asked, her eyebrows a deeply knitted unibrow. "Honestly, that's messed up. I don't blame JZ for leaving. He stood up for you today. We all did."

Brian tapped her hip.

Mina could feel his head, over hers, softly shaking side-to-side, warning her to let it go. She ignored it. "Seriously, what could Raheem possibly say . . ."

"Mina, it's not like I can avoid him forever," Jacinta said. She brushed some sand off her pants leg and folded her arms.

Mina stood up only a few inches from Jacinta. She lowered her voice, out of respect, not wanting to call Cinny out.

"Cinny, I know you and Raheem's relationship is complicated. But he hit you tonight." Mina frowned. "Isn't that like the perfect reason for being done with him for good?"

The light in Jacinta's eyes blazed and Mina's stomach curled. She hadn't meant to, but she'd backed Jacinta into a corner.

She braced herself.

Sure enough, Jacinta's hands flew up to her hips as she fussed, "First of all, I can't avoid Raheem forever. I go home every other weekend. And none of y'all know . . ." Her voice broke for a second. She swallowed quickly and rushed on. "What it's like to sit home every weekend with nothing to do now that me and him not together." Jacinta looked over at Kelly then at Lizzie, challenging them. "Second of all, don't sit up here and tell me that if the same thing happened to one of y'all, you wouldn't give the person a chance to clear the air with you."

Mina folded her arms. Her mouth pursed in a frustrated pout. "I can tell you this, if Brian ever hit me there's not gonna be any air clearing."

"Don't bring me in this," Brian grumbled.

Lizzie and Kelly chuckled, low and nervous.

"That's easy to say when you not in the situation, Princess." Jacinta blew out a loud, frustrated sigh before regaining her composure. "Whatever. We already know we never see stuff the same." At that Jacinta's eyebrows raised high. "You're the one who always bright-siding it. So what if I'm letting Raheem say his peace? Isn't that the bright side, Mina? Maybe he's sorry and just wanna let me know that." She sneered, folding her arms tight against her chest, "Or bright-siding it only works when it's something *you* want real bad?"

Mina swallowed over the lump in her throat. She took a second to check her surroundings. Their confrontation was drawing peers from a few nearby clusters. She stepped closer to Jacinta, angry but still determined not to get loud.

"There *is* always a bright side to stuff. But to me, you're ignor-ing it."

Jacinta was unflinching. "So what's the bright side, Mina? Please, school me."

"You're the one who kept saying you wished Raheem would re-alize it's over between you." Mina's right eyebrow shot up. Her voice was thick with sarcasm. "I'm thinking it doesn't take a brain surgeon to figure out that the relationship is officially dead when somebody pimp-slaps you."

"He didn't pimp-slap me," Jacinta barked, causing a few more cu-rious squints from the surrounding clusters.

"Cinny, okay, I was just being funny." Mina shook her head, plead-ing. "You have a good reason for not talking to him. I hear what you're saying about letting him clear the air. But honestly . . ." Her shoulders hitched and her voice lost steam. "I think he said it all when he hit you."

"Well, that's your opinion," Jacinta said. She walked away, stop-ping only when she realized Kelly wasn't right behind her. "Kelly, come on."

Kelly stood frozen, unwilling to blatantly choose a side. Her voice was weak and unconvincing when she said, "It'll be okay, Mi," before walking off.

Mina watched until the darkness swallowed them.

"Woah, serious catfight," Todd said. "Mreow."

Lizzie tugged his arm. "Let's go for a walk."

Todd popped up. He rubbed Mina's arm. "She'll be alright, Mina.

You know Cinny's a tough cookie." He helped Lizzie up then back-pedaled into the sand. "I'll race ya."

Lizzie gave one wistful look back at Mina stewing, then hurried to catch up with Todd.

"Seriously, you gotta stop trying to fix everything," Brian said, softly reprimanding.

"I'm not trying to fix anything." Mina's voice went up a level. "But he smacked the spit out of her just a few hours ago . . ." She blew out a resigned breath. "Whatever."

Let the Circle Be Unbroken

"I don't argue like this with anyone but you."
—Corrine Bailey Rae, "Like A Star"

Jacinta felt like she and Kelly were walking from one world into another, leaving the shadowy, loud beach scene for the bright but silent world of the hotel's parking lot. The whish of passing cars on the nearby highway was quiet compared to the crashing waves, layered conversations and thin music of the party. She found the near silence nerve-wracking.

In spite of her anxiety, her legs sped up. Once out of the sand, her feet clomped loudly on the sidewalk. She jumped at the sound of Kelly's, "Are you okay?" and bit back the urge to snap, *Yes, stop asking me that.*

Everyone was concerned for her. Just being a friend. Having her back. She got it.

As cool as it was having four and five people giving you big pity eyes and lowering their voices as they checked on your sanity, it was also bothersome. She was so used to it being just her, Raheem and Angel that the clique's attention and concern was smothering.

Their concern was what Raheem called, being all in her business.

Times like now she agreed with him. Then she glanced over at Kelly. There was nothing but genuine worry in her friend's light-brown eyes, shaming Jacinta's annoyance away. She slowed her steps. "I'm fine. For real."

"You know I would have told you they were coming down here if I'd known. Right?" Kelly asked.

Jacinta nodded. She knew that, but couldn't help lecturing. "If you had told me Angel knew about the road trip, then I could have told you there was no way you were gonna keep him away."

The confusion on Kelly's face amused Jacinta.

"But I told him it was just the girls." Kelly squinted in concentration as she recollected. "He seemed okay with it being a girls' thing."

"Kelly, I have never seen Angel so pressed as he is with you. You got that knucka completely open . . ." Jacinta shook her head. "He probably had the car gassed up right after he talked to you."

They both chuckled.

Angel's Acura was at the curb near a sign that said BEACH EN-TRANCE. Raheem leaned against the car, his head turned toward Angel inside the car. They hadn't seen the girls. Kelly stopped abruptly and lowered her voice, even though they weren't in hearing range of the guys.

"How come you didn't tell us that you and Raheem still hook up?"

Jacinta's eyes lowered. She looked away from Kelly and over at the guys. They still hadn't seen them.

We should head back to the beach like we never bothered to come, Jacinta thought.

"Cinny?" Kelly prodded.

Jacinta's shoulders heaved. No matter how much she explained her and Raheem's relationship to the girls they never seemed to totally understand. She wasn't angry with Kelly but she didn't feel like explaining again. Instead she said, "It's not like I hate him, Kell."

"I know," Kelly said. Her voice was thick with sympathy. "But . . . okay, I'm not saying you're to blame for what Raheem did . . ."

Jacinta rolled her eyes. "Which means you are saying that."

"What do you mean?" Kelly tucked her hair then head-checked the guys, deep in conversation.

"You're gonna say that I'm leading him on or sending him mixed signals or whatever."

Kelly was apologetic. "Well . . . aren't you? Kind of?"

"It's not like it happened every time I went home." Jacinta frowned. "Just a couple . . . I mean like three times." She blew out an exasperated breath. "And Raheem knew it didn't mean we were back together."

"What did it mean?"

"I don't know." Jacinta renewed her fast-paced stride. "Let's just . . . get this over with."

Angel was already teasing Jacinta by the time Kelly reached the car. He greeted Kelly with a smile. "Ay, hop in, mami."

Jacinta saw Kelly calculating whether to go or stay. "It's cool," she said, letting her off the hook.

Kelly reluctantly headed to the passenger side, her eyes never leaving Jacinta's face. Jacinta watched the car pull off until it was a tiny speck of taillights.

Once Angel's Acura was out of sight, Raheem moved in closer.

"Un-ah," Jacinta warned, taking a step back. "I only came out here because I don't want you thinking I'm running or scared of you."

He put his hands up, no tricks up his sleeve, then gestured to the retaining wall around the hotel's garden. They both sat down.

He sucked his teeth when Jacinta left plenty of room between them, then delivered his apology in classic Raheem style—one part gruff, one part genuine.

"Man, look . . . I'm sorry I hit you. For real."

"You mean you're just sorry." Jacinta folded her arms tighter and glared. "That's what you used to say about your father. That he was sorry and trifling for hitting on your moms."

Her heart galloped when Raheem's jaw tightened and his nose flared.

She silently counted the seconds as they went by.

One one thousand. Two one thousand. Three one thousand.

The anger which had brought on the hurtful (but true) shot gave way to teeming anxiety.

Twenty-five one thousand. Twenty-six one thousand.

She'd gone too far, but wasn't worried about Raheem striking her again. They were out in a well-lit parking lot with people walking by every few seconds. She was more worried about not being able to take the words back.

Forty one thousand.

Raheem hated his father. Her comparing him to the man who his mom had finally kicked out two years ago, was as much a knife in the heart as it would be if Raheem threw Jacinta's mother being a drug addict in her face. She braced herself for something hurtful to come her way.

At the fifty-five second mark, Raheem spoke up, his voice vanilla and emotionless. "That's messed up that you went there . . . but I was straight wrong for hitting you, so I deserve it." He scooted closer to her, waited for her to scoot away. When she didn't, his body relaxed. "Cinny, let's stop playing each other and talk straight up."

"About what? Nothing's changed." Her eyebrows raised in a sharp spike, questioning.

Raheem's eyes went glassy, as if thinking about it. Finally he said, "Exactly, nothing's changed. I still love you." He closed the final gap of space between them so their legs touched. For a second the chill from the cool wall was held off by their body heat. Raheem's fingers stroked her upper thigh. "Real talk. You messing with Jason?"

Jacinta shook her head.

"So why was you all up on him then?"

The pain in Raheem's voice melted the last of Jacinta's fragile resolve. The same thing that happened when she came home on the weekends was happening again.

Worse, because his hard edge was smoothed over by his gentle touch. She wanted to believe. And she wanted to run—far away from his brown eyes, heavy with regret, silently saying things to her that he would probably never admit out loud. Like, he missed her and wanted her back.

She cleared her throat. "I still love you too. But . . ."

"Why it gotta be a but?" he asked softly, almost apologetically.

"Because it's too hard, Heem." It killed her to say it. But she pressed on. "You act like you're mad that I'm happy. The only time it's swazy is when I'm doing what you want me to do. But that sucks for me."

Raheem barked a loud laugh. He mocked her voice. "That sucks for you?"

Jacinta's mouth pursed. "Yeah, that sucks for me."

He nudged her. "I'm just playing with you, girl. You gon' sit there and tell me that you saying *that sucks for you* is not white? It sounds funny coming from you. That's all."

Of course it sounded white to him. She had never used the word "sucks" until hanging around Mina and the clique. Jacinta's cheeks burned with embarrassment. Not at using the word, but at Raheem pointing it out and laughing. She played it off by shrugging.

"Come on, Cinny. *Sucks?*" he pressed, wanting her to admit it.

"Alright, alright. It's not like I walk around using it all the time," she said, standing up to face him. "But that's what I mean. Little things like that. You're always teasing how I talk. Or being all sarcastic when I tell you what we did on the weekends, like it's wack. It's played out."

"So if I stop teasing you we cool?"

"It's not just that, Heem." Jacinta's voice rose. She was pleading again and hated it. But it was too late. "On the few weekends that you and Angel came over to The Woods and hung out with us, I thought it was cool. It seemed like y'all had a good time. But then the next time we talked you joked me about stuff I said or did while you were there. It's like I have to watch what I say or do. It's foul."

"'Cause I hate that you . . . it's like you have more fun when you with them or something." Raheem's lip jutted in a pout. "And everything is Mina and 'nem this and Mina and 'nem that. I just get mad sick of hearing it."

Jacinta matched his pout. "And that's why nothing has changed."

"But what if I tried?" Raheem pulled her toward him by the forearms. His voice was all gentle, no gruff. "For real. I'm gonna try harder."

As he pulled, Jacinta had to straddle his legs to go forward. Soon she was standing just inches from his face. Her heart raced, but it was heavy. She'd never wanted to say no, and yes, so badly.

They'd done this already. They'd tried to make it work. Every time it went bad, it went really bad. She wasn't up for the ride anymore, but then Raheem winked at her. His voice was sincere and smooth when he said, "You know you my down-ass chick."

"I'm not gonna apologize for having fun without you, Heem," Jacinta said. But it was a weak, empty statement. His arms were around her waist, locking her in against him.

"Alright," he said.

"And don't get all pissy when I say I need help out one of my friends," Jacinta scolded.

He nodded.

"And stop teasing me. I'm not acting white."

Raheem chuckled softly. "Cinny, I don't tease you no more than always. You just mad sensitive now."

The truth in his words took Jacinta back. Instead of admitting he was right, she added on more rules until she couldn't think of anything else to say. "And . . ."

"Do I need to sign a contract or something?" Raheem teased.

He looked straight into Jacinta's eyes, unflinching, waiting for her to give more conditions. Jacinta made herself meet his gaze. She searched his eyes for something, anything that would tell her that getting back with him was the right thing to do.

It felt right and it felt wrong.

Her brain was foggy. Details about the bad times between them were already hazy as she looked into his eyes.

She loved him.

He was her first.

She mostly loved being around him.

He'd always been there for her . . . the "right" list kept growing, passing the "wrong" by a mile.

"One more thing," Jacinta said, finally.

Raheem cocked his head. "I'm listening."

She patted his crazy afro. "Let me braid this nest . . . like, now."

"Oh, I'm not looking sexy?"

"Yeah, to some chick who like that Ben Wallace, mean mug look."

"That's not you, huh?"

Jacinta shook her head.

A smile lit Raheem's handsome face, softening the hard, ragged look of the afro. He moved his face in and kissed her.

Jacinta wrapped her arms around his neck, letting the familiar comfort settle over them.

This is right, she thought.

As long as Raheem tried, really tried, it would be just like . . . her phone beeped twice, signaling she had a text.

"That's probably your girl Mina wondering if I dragged you off in the woods somewhere."

Jacinta sucked her teeth. "Not funny. Leave my girl alone."

"Shawty bucked like she was ready knuck." Raheem chuckled,

like Mina getting in his face was the most amusing thing he'd ever seen. Admiration laced his words. "She had your back, for real. She cool peoples."

Jacinta smiled, nodding as she opened the phone to check the text.

"Yeah. That's my . . . aw, shoot."

Good-bye to the Game?

"Said goodbye to the game, but I'm still wavin'."
—Playaz Circle ft. Lil Wayne, "Duffle Bag Boy"

Angel cruised the Acura down the highway. He gazed at Kelly. She sat arms folded, head ducking in the passenger side mirror, looking back at the hotel, uptight.

Angel pinched her arm playfully. "They'll be alright."

Seeing a cloud pass over her face, he assured her again in Spanish as he rolled the car along lazily in the light traffic.

"Has he ever hit her before?" Kelly stared Angel down, wanting to see his face for any sign that whatever answer he gave was true or false.

"No. He was pissed." Angel shook his head. "He knew he was mad foul."

"Yeah, right," Kelly muttered.

"Do you think Cinny would have came out here to talk to him if this wasn't the first time?" Angel took his eyes off the road for a second and glanced Kelly's way. Bars of light from passing street lamps zebra'd across her face, etched with concentration. "Kelly, you saw her clock him back, right? Trust, it was the first time."

True, Kelly thought. It may have taken Jacinta a second, but she responded in true Jacinta fashion. Her shoulders relaxed. "So, where are we going?"

"Just riding to give them some time."

"Not trying to start anything . . ." There was an unspoken apology in her shrug. "But I wish you had told me you were coming down."

"Yeah, well I wish you would have told me that Cinny and dude had something going."

"They don't," Kelly said, sure to keep the bite out of her voice.

Angel's eyebrows shot up. "She was sitting on his lap, Kelly. Man, when Heem saw that he rolled up on them so quick . . . it was a bad look. Cinny was wrong."

"You know what?" Kelly looked out her window, steamy with moisture. She watched the fog disappear before facing Angel again. "I don't see how we're going to be together if Raheem and Jacinta aren't. I mean . . . he's your friend. Jacinta's mine. We'll never be able to hang out together."

"You act like they not both my friends too." He frowned for a second before giving in to the stubborn jut in Kelly's lip. "Alright, so we won't always hang out together."

"If you really felt that way you would have come down here by yourself." Kelly winced at the nagging in her voice and waited for Angel to get testy with her.

Instead, he rubbed her cheek. He gave her one of his shy but devilish, I'm-a-bad-boy smiles. "Alright, my bad. But, real talk, if you had just told me that . . . never mind. You're right. Knowing how Raheem and Cinny back and forth, I should have looked out better than that."

Kelly smiled. "See. It's not so bad when you admit I'm right."

Angel's hazel eyes crinkled with a smile even though he sucked his teeth.

He leaned over, hovering over the middle console, his lips pursed. "Give me some."

Kelly shooed him away. "Drive before we crash."

"I can do more than one thing at a time." He leaned further over and the car swerved with his motion. He tapped his cheek. "Just a little kiss, right there."

The car veered more to the right as Angel horsed around.

"Angel, seriously," Kelly said, on the edge of panic. "Stop playing, please."

She saw the blue lights before she heard the siren. They filled the little Acura, washing it in swirling white and blue. But the loud "whoooop" still made her jump out of the seat.

Angel cursed, muttering as he dug in his pocket. A small, tightly wrapped ball of plastic was between his fingers. He shoved it at Kelly, dropping it in her lap. "Take this. Put it in your purse."

Kelly picked up the dark, greenish ball then dropped it like it was on fire.

"What is it?"

"Put it in your purse," Angel demanded. Keeping his body as straight as possible, he reached his arm over and opened the dash, plucked out several more plastic balls and dropped them on her lap. "Just do it." His demand turned to pleading. "Please, nenesita."

Kelly turned to look through the back window. She could make out the outline of a police cruiser through the darkness.

"Don't turn and look," Angel barked. He cursed under his breath again. His shoulders rose then fell as he took a deep breath. He slowed the car down and pulled over to the curb. His words spilled out in a rush. "Kelly, look, just put it in your purse. Alright? It'll be cool. I promise. Just . . . just be calm."

"I don't have a purse," she said through clenched teeth. She folded her arms and challenged Angel with a "so what now," look.

His eyes bugged with panic for a fleeting second. He looked Kelly over then nodded his head to the bottom pocket on the leg of her capri cargo pants. "In your pocket. Put it in that little pocket."

Kelly shook her head. "This is unbelievable. I can't . . ."

A bright spotlight shone into the car, cutting off her words.

"Your pocket, nenesita," Angel urged. He turned his face to the front of the car and put both hands on the steering wheel.

Only moving her arms, Kelly placed the four balls in the pocket beside her knee. Tears of fury welled in her eyes.

Me and my mother, two peas in a pod, good girls with bad boys, she thought before realizing her mind had gone there. The thought made her eyes itch as the unshed tears fought to drip. She fought them back.

We're not alike, she told herself.

She thought Angel had stopped. Had made him stop. She wasn't like her mother. She'd done the right thing. She would have never . . .

There was a clink-clink at the window as the officer motioned for Angel to put the window down.

Kelly stared at the buttons on the officer's shirt. She gasped as the buttons were replaced with the officer's square-jawed, clean shaven, unsmiling face looking into the car.

"Everything alright in here?" he asked, a slight twang making the last word "he-ah."

"Yes, sir," Angel said. He faced the officer but kept his hands on the wheel.

It made Kelly sick to her stomach that he knew the drill.

She'd never been stopped by a policeman her entire life. Grand drove the speed limit, wore her seatbelt and was a squeaky clean driver. Kelly's heart felt like it had stopped. She held her breath, afraid to let it go for fear the policeman would become suspicious. She let the breath out in slow, soft puffs and let the officer's strange drawl distract her.

"I was behind *yew* for the last three minutes." The officer's neck stretched forward. He took inventory with his eyes as he informed Angel, "*Yew* were swerving. Didja know that, sir?"

"Yes, sir," Angel said. "I was . . ."

"*Yew* two been drinking?" He cocked an eye over at Kelly then took one step back from the window, not bothering to wait on an answer. "Come on out, son."

Kelly kept her eye on the scene as the officer gave Angel a sobriety test.

Please, please say he and Raheem haven't been drinking, Kelly prayed.

She held her breath as Angel walked a straight line, touched his arms to his nose then back out wide. He seemed to be okay. Kelly couldn't really tell. The officer's face was stern, revealing nothing.

She caught the words "playing around"—that was Angel—and "know better . . . you kids," from the policeman. It wasn't until she heard "warning," that the air escaped her like a balloon losing helium.

Within seconds, Angel was back in the car. He waited until the shadow of the cop walking back to his cruiser passed his window before pulling the car back into the slow-moving traffic that had formed as cars instinctively slowed down for the flashing lights.

Kelly folded her arms. She stared straight ahead, ears and face on fire, her head heavy.

She refused to bawl outright. Instead, the tears came slow, hot and silent.

Angel had lied to her. And he'd made her hold his . . . at the thought she reached into her pocket. Her fingers slid over the plastic balls as she tried to grip them. She used her free hand to wipe her running nose and slowed down the other hand until it palmed the plastic balls. She snatched them out then threw them over at Angel.

Her blood pressure soared when he said, "Nenesita, I'm sorry," in his seductive romantic thug lilt.

Her eyes popped wide and the tears streamed faster. *Sorry? That's all he was going to say?* she thought. If this was a bad dream she needed to wake up now before she screamed and woke up the whole house.

But it wasn't.

Angel was looking at her, his hazel eyes pleading for understanding. Waiting on her to say . . . what? *Okay, it's totally fine that you just made me shove drugs in my pocket?*

She turned away from him, furious. "Angel, just take me back . . . please." She spat the last word like it angered her to use it.

When her Sidekick tinkled, she didn't know whether to be glad or bothered by the distraction. She eased it out of her front pocket and flipped it open, expecting an angry text from Mina wondering where they were. She frowned, wiped at her eyes and moved the Sidekick closer to her face.

"Extreme Skank?" she muttered, confused, then gasped when she saw the pictures.

Extreme Skank

"Men don't want no hot female, that's been around the
block female."
—Destiny's Child, "Nasty Girl"

It didn't matter that Brian's chest was pressed against her back,
warming her against the ocean's breezy chill. Or that she had another ninety minutes of social life left before her parents brought
down what would no doubt be the ultimate punishment. Or that
Lizzie and Todd were the world's cutest shadows walking hand in
hand near the water's edge. All Mina could think about was Jacinta
and JZ.

She nodded and threw in a few "un-huh's" at Brian's attempts to
move on, her eyes wandering, staring off into the night, picking out
JZ, then Lizzie, then back to JZ.

JZ's feelings were hurt. Not that he'd ever admit it. He didn't
have to. Mina knew it as soon as he hopped up talking about checking out girls. Whether she liked it or not, JZ and Jacinta's flirting had
turned to something more, even if neither of them admitted it. In
Mina's opinion, Jacinta going to hear Raheem out, or whatever she
wanted to call it, was an insult to JZ. Sympathy for him pricked her
heart.

He'd shaken it off, carousing and hopping from circle to circle of
people talking and . . . he had a red cup in his hand, so drinking too.

He'd come back to the blanket three times, each time louder and more animated than the last.

The third time, to Mina's horror, he'd asked Brian if he needed any "protection."

All she could do was whisper-shout, "Jay!" hoping he'd at least lower his voice.

But Brian had chuckled, given JZ a pound and said, "Naw, player, I'm good. You better take it easy, spilling like that."

"I'm good, son," JZ said. Mina had shaken her head as his feet got caught in the cheer blankets and he tripped but didn't fall as he walked off.

Then there was Jacinta, the reason JZ was already loudly inebriated.

Mina didn't know whether to be mad or feel sorry for her. Every time she'd chosen a side, a new thought changed her mind. She was leaning back toward mad when Brian pushed himself up.

She looked up in confusion.

How long had she been dazing?

Brian's hand loomed in front of her. She took it and let him pull her into a standing position.

"Let's walk," he said.

They made their way through the thick clusters of partyers to the water's edge and walked the opposite direction of Lizzie and Todd. Brian softly squeezed her hand. The electricity raced to her fingers and Mina's grip relaxed, letting Brian's hand completely enclose hers. They walked in silence until the party was nothing more than dark shadows, dimmed kerosene lamps and cell phone ghost lights.

Away from the crowd, the ocean crashing against the shore took its rightful place as the loudest sound in the night. The silence took Mina back to the night before, and Brian's request to be honest with him about how she felt. Sudden shyness took over.

The moon shone bright on the beach, sandwiching them between the heavy darkness of the endless ocean and the string of ho-tels' speckled lighting on the other. She glanced over at him, able to see every feature of his face in the moon's light.

A wave of happy bubbles floated in her stomach, loosening her tongue. "So, are you mad at me?"

"No. Why?"

She raised her voice to be heard over the waves. "Because of what I said to Cinny."

Brian's eyebrows jumped, just a little. "No." There was a "but" at the end of his short sentence and Mina, in an uncharacteristic show of patience, waited for him to finish. Twenty seconds later he stopped walking and turned to her. "I just don't get why you think you always need to jump in and help."

"Okay, you did see Raheem slap her, right?" Mina folded her arms against the breeze whipping off the water. Irritation rose in her chest.

Brian's chest rose and fell in a soft rhythm. He chose his words carefully. "Yeah, I saw it. It was foul . . . and . . . I mean, that's your girl. So I understand why you ran to help her out. I'm not saying that was wrong."

"Then what *did* I do wrong?" Mina's eyebrows arched.

"I'm not trying to argue with you, toughie." Brian rubbed her arms. A smile tugged at his mouth and the corner of his eyes.

Hearing the nickname he'd given her for being so headstrong al-ways softened her. She closed the space between them, walking into Brian's arms. He wrapped them around her and she soaked in his scent before looking up at him. "I'm just trying to have my girl's back."

"Word. I'm with that," Brian said.

"But?"

He laughed. "But, sometimes you just need let it play out and then be there for your girl on the back end." He shrugged. "That's all I'm saying."

"Fine." She buried her face in his shirt, her voice muffled. "So I should just be there when Raheem pimp-slap her again?"

She looked up into his laughing face and smiled.

"I didn't say all that." Brian moved his face down to hers. "Do you, toughie. I ain't mad."

Mina eagerly met him halfway as their faces collided softly, ending in a kiss. They kissed slow, relishing each second in a way they couldn't at school or when Mina's parents were hanging out in the next room. Brian pulled away. He held her chin between his thumb and forefinger. "Don't take this wrong, alright?"

"What? The kiss?" Mina asked, dazed.

Why? It was fuggin' awesome, she thought, lost in the way Brian's mouth tasted like cinnamon Altoids. She hated the things, they were too hot, but they tasted good—mildly spicy—on his mouth and made her tongue tingle.

"Naw." Brian's chuckle was soft, ironic as if he still wasn't used to some of the crazy things that came out of Mina's mouth. He kept his face close to hers as he said, "Don't take it wrong when I ask, for the next hour we don't talk about Jacinta or JZ or anybody else."

Mina giggled. "That wasn't a question."

"Exactly." He kissed her again, squeezing her closer to him for a second before letting go. He led her back to the sandy, darkened part of the beach and they sat, her between his legs again, leaning back on his chest.

The night was turning cold. Sitting in the cooling sand made it even colder. But a snowstorm wouldn't have sent Mina inside a second before ten forty-five. She wriggled deeper against Brian's chest when he put his arms around her, shielding her from some of the cool air.

Mina sighed, a mix of contentment and sadness. "You do realize that I'm so punished when I get home, right?"

Brian nuzzled her neck. "Yup. Want take bets on how long?"

She sucked her teeth. "Not even funny . . . but, I'm thinking at least a month."

"Da-yum, for real?" Brian's arms squeezed her. "So can I date other chicks or what?"

Mina's head whipped against his chest as she turned to look up at him. "See, I know you think that's funny, but I d-o-n-t."

His laughter startled a couple walking by.

"My b-a-d. At least you won't be by yourself. Your girls be on lockdown with you."

"True." Mina pondered out loud, "As long as the 'rents at least let me have internet access . . . I can get through this."

"Um-huh, then I can still send you nasty IMs."

She smacked at his knees, embarrassment warming her cheeks. She almost found herself thinking maybe punishment would be a good thing, help slow things down a little—help them keep that brand-new couple feeling. But Brian's lips were on her neck, making her toes curl. The thought of slowing down was crushed by alarms going off in her brain as it sang, *God, this feels good. God, this feels good. God, this feels GOOD.*

Mina jumped, startled when her phone vibrated and Brian's blared T-Pain's "Buy U A Drank," at the same time. She'd ignored the last five times it buzzed. This time she dug into her jacket pocket as Brian lifted himself up and took his cell out of his back pocket. They both flipped their phones open at the same time.

"I got a text," they chorused.

"Jinx! Buy me . . ." Mina stopped short when she opened the message titled Extreme Skank and saw herself lip locked with Craig.

Only the ocean made a sound as she and Brian both stared down at the pic on their phones, silent.

In a way, Mina wasn't surprised to see the photos. There were two. As she gaped at them, her brain cells split into two camps, the "well, you should have known betters" and the "not agains."

Deadly silent behind her, Brian's chest heaved up and down, up and down, first slow, then a little faster every second he stared wordlessly at his phone.

As seconds ticked by without him uttering a word, her heart crawled to the base of her throat, threatening to walk right out of her mouth.

Mina grilled the pictures. Someone had caught one of her and Craig face-to-face, but not kissing. It was grainy and shadowy, but Mina recognized it. She'd been falling out of one of the wobbly guy stunts and was ready to topple completely over Craig's head when he'd reached his arms up and basically plucked her out of the sky instead of really catching her. It was an awkward, clumsy catch. Her back had the shirt burn to prove it.

Whoever (Jessica) had taken it, had a flash on their cam phone, but it hadn't done a good job of combating the beach's darkness. The two shadows could have been anyone. Mina could have totally pleaded innocence on that one.

It was the kissing pic that was the killer. The image was crystal clear and by some strange twist of fate or technology, while her face hadn't been easily identifiable—too covered by Craig's—the blue ribbon she'd been wearing in her hair, with BubbliMi in gold letters, jumped off the picture, daring her to pull that old "it's not me" bull.

She ignored Brian's silence and rapid breathing for as long as she could before standing up and blurting, "It's not what you think."

"It's not a picture of you and Craig kissing?" Brian stared up at her, his usually smiling eyes not.

The spit fled Mina's mouth at the dryness in his voice. The underlying accusation, naked and matter-of-fact, was worse than if he had yelled or been sarcastic. She had no idea how to answer the question, since obviously it was exactly what it looked like.

Her tongue stuck to the roof of her mouth. "It's Jessica," she said, every word accompanied by a weird clicking sound as her tongue dislodged itself each time.

And before Brian could say what his eyes were already shouting Mina turned heel, hot-footing it back to the party, the sudden urge to confront Jess a living ball of fear, anger and resignation.

Upper Hazing

"Hey, you, I don't like your girlfriend."
—Avril Lavigne, "Girlfriend"

Jessica had watched Mina and Brian walk off into the darkness and waited, giving them a chance to savor their alone time. At the time, a delicious sense of satisfaction filled her chest as she wondered how Mina would untangle herself out of this and bright-side it.

There'd been dozens of Extreme Moments sent since yesterday's Individual & Partner stunt performance. People had been caught in some kooky, posed positions from Thursday night at Guidos, and even crazier candid shots from last night—some people in even more compromising positions than Mina.

With every cell phone an automatic video cam, you'd think people would be more careful, Jess thought wryly.

The difference between Mina's photo and everyone else's was, that Jess had, of course, choreographed Mina's photo to perfection. Actually, it had ended up better than she'd expected. All she'd really done was talk Bo into getting Craig over to Mina's table. The best she'd hoped for was a close, cozy one of Mina grinning as usual. The whole kiss had been all Craig, a little extra windfall that had made its way into Jess's plan.

She squinted into the night and knew immediately that the shadowy speck heading briskly her way was Mina.

Let the fireworks begin, she thought, now weary and a little less happy than she'd been a few minutes ago, because the plan hadn't gone *totally* according to plan.

"Is that her?" Mari-Beth teetered on wobbly legs beside her. Her words slurred slightly from the syrupy concoction Breck had been feeding her all night.

Jess nodded, wrinkling her nose against the hum of alcohol on Mari-Beth's breath.

"If Brian breaks up with her, I'll have Breck put in a good word for you," Mari-Beth said. She nudged Jessica hard enough to make them both stumble. "He's so doable."

"Totally," Jess said without conviction.

She wasn't nearly as giddy as she'd hoped to be, watching Mina bee-line her way over, Brian trailing a good fifteen feet behind.

Even though Jess knew at least ten girls who would have paid her money to be in on the scheme that could put Brian James back on the market, right in time for his senior year, she'd only intended to send the photos to Brian and Mina. Make Mina sweat, cause a little couples tension, ruin their spring break, basically send the message, *watch your back when you're dating a hottie.*

But Mari-Beth had overruled her, insisting they send it to everyone as an Extreme Moment. "What, are you getting soft on me? God, Jess," Mari-Beth had sneered when Jess reminded her that the kiss pic was a private joke—only the grainy, cozy photo was meant as an Extreme Moment.

But MB had snatched the phone from Jess and instructed the other Glams to help pass both photos along.

Jess hadn't had much time to think of the consequences of the massive text. She wasn't worried about Mina so much as Sara. She'd promised Sara it was a real truce, a lie Jess could easily uphold had she only sent the kiss pic to Mina and Brian. But one that would be increasingly hard to hide now, depending on how Mina handled it.

She dreaded the cold shoulder she'd get from Sara over this, but blocked it out.

It's just a little Upper hazing. Everyone's gone through it, Jess told herself, putting on her game face. She wanted to teach Mina a lesson, well here it was—trust no one.

She watched as Mina, only a few feet away, raced like a heat-seeking missile that's found its target.

Brian's stride was long and lazy.

They were clearly on the outs.

Mission accomplished . . . kind of.

The Truce: Fade to Black

"You didn't need to treat me that way."
—Maroon 5, "Wake Up Call"

Mina's eyes were glossy, blurring her vision. She stumbled in the cold, lumpy sand, not caring if she fell. Her long stride and set face left no doubt that she was about to confront someone. Sensing the drama to come, the clusters of people broke up, gravitating slowly toward the kerosene lamps. Some people casually idled closer to the center, while others openly trailed behind Mina, curious.

By now they'd looked at the pictures long enough to distinguish who was in them. A few people, anticipating her direction, gathered near Craig and shot eager looks Brian's way—maybe a fight was on the horizon. But they were disappointed when Mina walked by Craig without a second glance.

A full twenty feet from Mina, Brian was quickly swallowed in the crowd as the loose circle of partyers became a tight fight circle. By the time Mina finally reached Jessica, the party was officially a spectator event.

Brian pushed his way to the front, but made no moves to get any closer than it required to keep a clear field of vision.

In anger, Mina's voice was squeaky, as if she'd lost the ability to control it. "Way to set me up, Jess."

Jess's voice was calm, full of mock innocence. "Mina, all I did was *take* the picture. You starred in it." Jess looked at Mari-Beth for backup. Relief crossed her face when an obviously intoxicated Mari-Beth gave it, nodding along, smug, her arms crossed.

"We've captured a few hundred Extreme Moments, Mina," Mari-Beth lectured, over-loud—the way of the drunken. "What's the big deal?"

Mina looked from Jess to Mari-Beth, unsure who to address. She hadn't anticipated having to take on both of them.

She chastised herself. She hated being hated and that need to be liked had played right into Jess's plan. Mina was sure there had been one. She was sick thinking how easily Jess had snagged her into the web.

Except for the perpetual crashing waves the beach was eerily quiet. Someone had turned down the music and Mina felt every single eye on her. The kerosene lamps felt like spotlights and she was center stage.

In the face of the Glam leaders, the rest of their flunkies flanking them to the left and right, the emotions that had fueled her walk over were gone, leaving her emotionally naked.

Mina took a hesitant glance around the tight circle. For the first time that night, she actually made out the faces of people. She blocked out the feeling of being under a microscope and focused. A few questions floated freely down her stream of consciousness—Did Jess talk Craig into kissing her? Was his apology a setup all for this? Was Bo in on it too? How many people did it take to make her look foolish? And how much of it was her fault?

She hushed the voice that asked the last question and concentrated on the first three.

When you knew the whole story behind her and Jess, they were perfectly sane questions. But out loud, Mina was sure they'd come off wrong.

In the pulsing glow of the kerosene lamps it was hard to read Jess's face. The smile in her eyes went from sincere to cunning, thanks to the shadow from twenty flickering flames.

When Mina finally spoke, the fight in her was a thin wisp of regret and anger. With the eyes of the spectators probing her back, her words came out a petulant whine. "You didn't have to call me a skank."

Jessica's face was haughty, a reminder that Mina was new to these parts of town, clueless to the protocol. With a sense of finality, Jess schooled her. "This is what it's like to roll with the big girls, Mina." She swished her hair and the cunning/friendly glint returned.

Just as Mina was about to accept, however reluctantly, that this could definitely be construed as a gesture of acceptance in Jessica's mind, Jess's eyes flickered to Mina's left and she said, out of the blue, in a softer tone, "It was only a joke, anyway."

For a second, Mina was taken back by the near-apology.

"It was a stupid joke, Jess," Sara said, suddenly beside Mina. "As usual, you and the mod squad have to take everything too far."

A ripple of laughter made its way from the front of the crowd to the back and back to the front again. It wasn't every day that the Glams were openly mocked.

Mina could have kissed Sara. She stood a little straighter, relieved that someone else suspected the picture was more than an innocent Extreme Moment joke.

Sara and Jess held one another's gaze, making some sort of twin connection. Regret or fear passed like a ghost in Jess's eyes before steely resolve replaced it.

Mari-Beth frowned at Sara, but in lieu of any smart remark she rolled her eyes and waited for Jess to answer.

"Hey, all I did was take it. Mina was the one who took it too far," Jess maintained, her tone cranky but not nearly as "that's that" final. She addressed her last statement to the crowd more than to Sara. But no one backed her up, sending Jess to her soapbox. "Out of all the pictures we've sent, no one has said anything until now." She broke the gaze with her twin and the act gave her confidence. Arms folded tightly against her chest, she raised her voice as she polled the spectators, "Is anyone else tripping over their pics? Jake? Annie? Chandra?"

Mari-Beth giggled and called out a few more names of those whose Extreme Moments had ranged from gross to just short of illegal.

There were murmurs of discussion throughout the clusters, but no one objected. Jess's eyebrow arched in a "see, it's you."

"The subject line was wack," Mina said lamely, embarrassed.

"I guess it's a good thing we didn't use the original one," Mari-Beth said to Jess, then raised her voice to be heard, "Extreme H to da O."

She laughed and the Glams cackled along. There were titters from the crowd, but realizing there would be no fight, people had begun to trail off into individual conversations and break up into smaller groups.

"Lighten up, Mina," Mari-Beth snorted. "Or maybe next time keep all your PDA on the down low."

There was some laughter from the few spectators still paying attention.

"I wasn't . . ." Mina started and realized it was pointless. With the crowd thinning, her anger flickered fresh, dampened but alive. She stepped closer to Jess and Mari-Beth, and lowered her voice, uninterested in being a spectacle any longer. "If it was a joke, I guess you got me good because Brian's really hot with me now."

"And that's my fault how?" Jess asked, eyebrow raised.

Sara stepped in. The four of them made their own little cluster, blocking out any stragglers still listening.

"Did you set Craig up to do this?" Mina whispered angrily.

Sara's eyes bugged. "Jess, did you?"

"No," Jessica snorted. Her eyes cut to Mari-Beth, nervously.

Mari-Beth wore her bored look, checking her cell phone as if expecting it to ring any second to save her from the played-out conversation.

Jess forced a casual tone as she said, "I was just as surprised as you when Craig did that. It was too perfect not to get on film."

Mina stared into Jess's eyes, looking for the lie. But she couldn't trust her instincts. The shadows from the lamps were playing tricks on her. And either she was crazy or Jess seemed nervous and anxious.

"But you didn't have to send it to everybody," Sara pointed out.

"Oh, I'm sure Brian will get over it," Mari-Beth said dismissively. She stumbled away and returned to her clique, signaling to Jess that she'd had enough.

Jess glanced over Mina's shoulder at Brian. He stood his ground amidst the clusters, hands in his pants pockets, waiting for Mina, his face expressionless.

"What happened to the truce?" Sara whispered. Her eyebrows knitted into angry caterpillars, an odd look on her usually pleasant cocoa face. "I thought you guys were cool for the whole break."

Jessica matched Sara's whisper, infusing it with the right mix of confidence and indignation. "I already said it was a joke, Sara. I didn't violate the truce." Jess flashed a picture from her cell phone at her sister, of two girls, one the Homecoming Queen, kissing. "Hello, am I supposed to apologize to every single person we took a pic of?" Her grin was snide. "I'm pretty sure Heather's not going to be happy to see this pic next to the ones in her crown on Myspace. But that's her problem, not mine."

Sara scowled. "Then at least go tell Brian it was a joke."

"Puh, yeah right." Jess rolled her eyes. "And tell him what? That Mina slipped on a pepperoni and fell on Craig's mouth?"

Mina spoke through tight jaws. "Never mind, Sara. I don't expect Jessica, of all people, to do me any favors. I'll handle my own business."

Jess's smile was hollow as she said, "There you go. Welcome to life on the pop side." She shrugged. "Shit happens."

"Yeah, especially when you plan for it to happen," Mina said.

"Just tell him the truth. You didn't kiss Craig, he kissed you," Jess said.

The sincerity in her voice shocked Mina. But before it registered, Mari-Beth's voice reached out of the darkness from behind Jessica, sharp and annoyed. "Jess, are you guys *still* talking?"

Jessica leaned in and took a breath to speak, when Mari-Beth's face, pinched and disapproving, appeared beside Mina. "Just be glad we didn't put the Extreme Ho title on it," Jess said.

"Exactly," Mari-Beth said, all toothy grin. "Mina, you're right, there *is* a bright side to everything."

She and Jess cackled crazily as they walked off toward the music, leaving Sara and Mina in muted silence.

It's a Wrap

"You and me, I can see us dying . . . are we?"
—No Doubt, "Don't Speak"

With no fight to spice things up and Mina's pictorial crime just one of many committed over the weekend, the party went back into full swing. Music pumped at full volume, drowning out the crashing waves. The only person who cared about the pictures now was Mina and . . .

She took a deep breath and finally turned around to face Brian. He hadn't moved a muscle since arriving in that spot.

Mina walked a few feet toward him then stopped, thinking he'd meet her halfway. But Brian made no move to close the two feet between them.

Mina's neck tensed. She bit the inside of her cheek raw, building the nerve to close the gap between them.

Sara touched her arm lightly and Mina jumped.

"I'm sorry," Sara said. "I really thought you and Jess would . . ."

"Me too," Mina admitted. She didn't know what Sara was about to say. Would be friends? Would get through a weekend without drama? It didn't matter. She was grateful for what she saw in Sara's eyes. She forced cheer into her voice. "At least I know where I stand with her. No big loss." She chewed anxiously at her cheek, wincing. "Not so sure if I have a boyfriend anymore though."

Mina hardly heard Sara's "good luck" as she moved toward Brian and her punishment for courting disaster by bothering to talk to Craig at all.

That reminded her. She snatched her phone out of her capri pocket, expecting it to be well past her curfew—why not, everything else was crashing in on her. There was twenty minutes of freedom left. Gathering her thoughts, she blew out a long, noisy exaggerated sigh and stepped to Brian. "Can we talk?"

He grunted and walked past her.

Unsure if the grunt was a yes or no, Mina followed tentatively. She was relieved when Brian staked out a spot in the darkness, away from the party and closer to the pier that led from the beach to the hotel.

He leaned against a wooden post and stared at her, his gaze dead of emotion.

"So talk," he barked, startling her.

Mina swallowed hard, thought about starting with her theory about being set up, then changed her mind. She settled on the truth, as lame as it was, hating herself for taking Jess's advice. "He kissed me. I didn't kiss him."

She quickly laid out the short version of the kiss, stumbling over her words as if under interrogation. The bitter anger in his eyes condemned her.

"So you were with him all night?" Brian asked.

"No." Mina forced herself to look into his eyes, fearing that if she didn't he'd think she was lying. She'd never seen them so black and cold. "He was only at the table with me for like fifteen minutes."

"This wasn't taken at no table, Mina." Brian thrust his phone, with the beach picture shining, toward her.

"We were stunting . . ." Mina pieced her thoughts together quickly and they tumbled out in a random mess. She thrust her hands in her jacket pocket to keep from fidgeting. "I mean, him and some of the other guys were trying to put up stunts. I was falling and he caught me. Craig I mean. It was a million other people standing there. We weren't alone. And . . ."

Brian cut her off. "But y'all *were* hanging out Thursday night?"

Mina nodded, feeling stupid that Brian cut to the chase so smoothly. In the end it didn't matter if she and Craig were only together for five minutes the night before. However long, it was frozen in two images that told whatever story the viewer wanted.

Brian snapped the phone shut and shoved it into his pocket. "Funny how you didn't mention that when you were talking about everything else that happened down here." He mocked Mina, imitating her using a ditzy-clueless girl voice. "I hung out with Sara and Jess. I missed y'all, though. We were tripping but it's not the same without y'all here." He snorted. "Naw, I guess it ain't the same. When I'm here you can't hang out with your boy, Craig."

Mina's stomach lurched. Panic swarmed in her head like a cloud of pesky gnats as Brian's words spilled on in an angry rant.

"When were you gonna get to the part about how old boy slipped you some tongue? Or did you forget 'cause that's just how you roll?"

Tears of frustration welled in Mina's eyes. "I . . ." Her phone rang. She instinctively pulled it out of her pocket and stared dumbly at the blurry numbers. She picked up and Lizzie's voice was cheerful balm for her frazzled nerves.

"Hey, Mi. Oh my God. Me and Todd walked like three miles." She laughed and Mina could hear Todd in the background mouthing off about something. Lizzie chattered on. "Where is everybody? We're near the party, but I don't see anybody. Where are you guys?"

Mina's voice was thick with tears. "At the hotel pier."

"What's wrong?" Lizzie asked, alarmed.

"I'll tell you later."

Mina hung up. She started to apologize for taking the call but Brian cut her off as soon as she inhaled to speak. "If he kissed you and it was all on him, why didn't you tell me?"

"Because then you would have rolled up on Craig and there would have been drama."

"So what, you got his back now?" Brian challenged.

"No," Mina yelped. She was frustrated that she couldn't express herself. She took a quick breath and dove in, mixing in her own theory. "I'm just saying, I didn't want you getting in a fight over this. Craig kissed me. It was stupid. He was being stupid. It wasn't . . . he was just wildin' out."

"So instead of you telling me so I could step to dude, you don't say anything?" Brian's voice trembled with restrained patience. "So I look like a punk then."

"I . . . no . . . I mean, I didn't mean . . ." Mina's brain couldn't think fast enough.

Both relief and a new wave of embarrassment washed over her when Lizzie and Todd reached them.

"Man, my dogs are barking," Todd crowed. He woofed like a dog then stamped his feet, pretending to hush the howling. "I think we were halfway to Del Rio Bay before we realized we walked too far."

"Hey, guys," Lizzie said, hesitantly. She looked from Mina to Brian, then back at Mina nervously.

"Where's JZ, Jacinta and Kelly?" Todd asked, looking around as if they were hiding in the nearby sand dunes.

Mina shrugged.

Brian sulked. He looked past Todd and Lizzie to the party.

Finally clued in to their silence, Todd asked, "Did we interrupt something?"

Brian snorted, "Naw, y'all cool." He pulled his phone out of his pocket so hastily Mina was surprised he didn't rip his pants. Glancing at the time, he announced snidely, "Your curfew ready to blow up, shorty. Y'all better head in."

Mina blanched, but Brian's attitude stung her into action.

"Liz, go ahead. I'll catch up," she said, her words rushed.

"Okay." Lizzie eyed Brian's clenched jaw warily. "I guess Cinny and Kelly might be on their way in already. I'll go meet them." She tugged at Todd and headed down the pier.

Before they were out of earshot, Mina pleaded, "Brian, look, I know you're mad but . . . I wasn't trying to make you look soft or anything." She pulled the cellie out just enough to see the time. Seven minutes. She rushed on. "I should have told you about it. I'm sorry. When it happened, I was surprised. But seriously he was just wildin' out and it seemed stupid to make a big deal out of it."

Brian chuckled, but there was no humor in it. "Is that the story you sticking with, shorty?"

Mina's stomach plunged another inch.

She'd never hated the word "shorty" as much as she did hearing it come from Brian's mouth. She stammered, "It's not a story. It's the truth."

Brian's gaze stayed on the party. When seconds passed without him saying anything, Mina finally turned and looked that way too.

Craig stood on the edge of a cluster no more than thirty yards from them. She had no idea how she could see that it was him, it was so dark. But she did, and she was certain Brian did too. As wrong as it felt to ask, she did anyway. "Are you going to say something to Craig?"

Brian laughed, loud and mean. "Why? You worried he might tell a different story?"

Her heart was stricken instantly at the thought of what Craig might say if Brian confronted him publicly. Nothing good would come of the two of them posturing to be head stud.

"No," she said, and realized it wasn't a lie. She wasn't just worried, she was straight-up petrified.

"You already made me look like Chauncy the Clown, Mina." Brian pulled his eyes away from Craig and stared down at her. "Even if I did step to him, at this point I look like the chump since I'm finding out the same time as everybody else that he's tippin' with my girl." He laughed again. "Naw, my bad. Everybody else already saw y'all together the other night."

"It's not like that. We're not creepin'," Mina said. "It's . . ."

Brian checked his phone again. "You better dip, shorty. The clock's ticking and you've got like five minutes."

Mina's heart did the fifty-yard dash, hurtling down the track at breakneck speed. Her brain raced along with it, fighting to find the right words to bring back the Brian that was reasonable.

But the usual smile in his eyes was hard. It scared Mina because it didn't look forced. Brian wasn't just pretending to be mad. There wasn't an ounce of forgiveness in his face.

"Brian, don't be like this," Mina begged.

Brian's eyebrows came together in a furry knot. "Like what?"

"I know what I did was wack but . . ."

"Naw, no but. What you did was wack. Period."

His eyes cut into her like glass, stopping Mina's words before they could form coherently. He flipped his phone shut and started back toward the party. "Alright, later."

"Brian," Mina called out, not sure what she was going to say.

Tears trickled down her face. For a second she considered throwing herself down at his feet and begging him to understand, to hear her out. She didn't care if she was late. She was already punished. What's another charge on top of the ones she'd already stacked? She'd stay out here all night if that's what it took.

But Brian didn't give her that choice. He stopped and waited a few seconds.

Mina stared pitifully at him, sending a kinetic apology through the air.

"What?" he barked.

"I'm sorry," Mina said, barely above a whisper.

"Yup," Brian said before strolling off.

Endings

"You're not gettin' till you're gettin' to me."
—Aly & AJ, "Potential Breakup Song"

Racing down the pier, Mina ran straight to Lizzie, Jacinta and Kelly and they took up the marathon together to the room. Hearts racing from running up five flights of stairs, they flew clumsily through the door, arriving with one minute to spare to a dark, empty room and a note taped to the TV from Mina's mother:

You better had been on time. Call me after you read this.

After checking in, they took their turns in the bathroom to wash off the beach's scent and settled in for the night to catch up. Except for Lizzie, everyone was cocooned in their gloomy thoughts.

Jacinta lay stretched across one bed on her stomach. Kelly sat beside her, cross-legged.

Lizzie stood at the mirror, braiding her hair.

Mina sat against the headboard on the other bed, her legs crossed at the ankles. Refusing to put her cellie down, she continued her ritual from the day before, double- and triple-checking the phone for a signal, willing Brian to call or text.

Kelly finally broke the chain of self-pity. She made sympathetic eyes at Mina. "Mi, he just needs time to cool off. If he doesn't call tonight it doesn't mean you guys are through."

Mina's throat itched at the word, "through." She pushed it away by switching subjects. "So is that really it for you and Angel?"

Kelly's mouth was a tight line as she nodded.

Jacinta and Mina exchanged a quick, "yeah right," with their eyes.

Famous last words, Mina thought. But wisely reserved comment, just in case it really wasn't over.

"Is this what I have to look forward to? All this back and forth, breaking up?" Lizzie asked, anxiously. Her fingers flew through her thick hair. She made eye contact with her friends in the mirror. Their long faces were all the answer she needed. "This sucks." She hesitated, not wanting to bask while her friends waded in BF issues, but needing to all the same. "But I feel so . . . everything is so good right now. What's the point if this is part of the package?"

Mina laughed in spite of the knot in her stomach. "I can't see you and Todd having these issues." She flashed a confident smile at Lizzie's image in the mirror. "You're all golly-gee-whiz and he's all, aw-shucks. What are y'all gonna fight about, who's the nicest?"

Jacinta hopped up and put her arm around Kelly. She made her voice sound silly and jokey like Todd's. "Lizzie, you're the sweetest."

Kelly giggled, "No, *you're* the sweetest, Todd."

"No, you," Jacinta insisted.

"No, you," Kelly said back.

They ducked, laughing, as Lizzie threw a headband at them.

"We're not that sweet," Lizzie said. She laughed. "Are we?"

"Shoot, so what if you are?" Mina said, her funk bubbling its way to the surface again. "Me, I'm a drama magnet."

"Yeah, you are," Jacinta agreed.

"Thanks a lot." Mina rolled her eyes. She snapped to attention when Jacinta said, "I told you not to trust Jessica, Mina. Girl is off her rocker, for real."

"I don't need you to point that out to me, Cinny," she said.

"Maybe you do, because look what happened."

Mina gazed down at her phone, checking for the signal as she answered, "I'm not going to go around not trusting people, making them prove themselves all the time."

Kelly shifted uncomfortably on the bed. She sat on the edge as if expecting a need to spring up any second. Her eyes darted to Lizzie, who put the finishing touches on her braid before joining Mina on the bed.

Jacinta's eyes bugged. "And she hasn't given you enough reason to distrust her, yet?" She folded her arms. "Come on, Mina. The knife isn't just in your back, it's poking through to the other side as she twists it."

Mina faltered, but only a second, before she shot back. "I know *you're* not talking about trusting the wrong person."

Lizzie groaned as Jacinta hopped off the bed and stood by the dresser, laser-beaming them with her scowl.

"It's been a long day. Don't you guys think it's a bad idea to talk about this now?" Lizzie asked, raising her voice to be heard over Jacinta's cry of, "I know you're not comparing my relationship with Raheem, which was all good until I moved to The Woods, with your messed up love/hate, hate to love straight-up wack relationship with Jessica?"

Lizzie tried again. "Seriously, we're only going to . . ."

"I'm not," Mina said matter-of-factly. She stopped at that, baiting Jacinta.

Jacinta fell for it.

"Then what are you saying?"

Mina crossed her arms. Her head wagged as she talked, making her look like she was doing some new, crazy dance. "That you're too smart to make such a dumb decision."

"Dumb?" Jacinta yelled. Her body snapped to attention as if she'd been struck.

Kelly popped up off the bed, anticipating Jacinta's outburst. She stood in the middle of the floor between the two beds and between the standing Jacinta and sitting Mina. Lizzie followed suit, nearly sliding off the bed as she scooted closer to the edge, blocking Mina from any sudden moves.

"Cinny, she didn't call you dumb." Kelly looked from Mina to Jacinta, an uneasy referee between her friends. "Right, Mi? You're not saying she's dumb."

"No, I'm not saying that," Mina said. "But going back with Raheem *is* a dumb thing to do."

"And trusting Jessica was a dumb thing to do," Jacinta spat. "And honestly, Mina, when somebody keeps doing dumb things they start looking dumb."

Mina recoiled as if she'd been smacked. "Are you calling *me* dumb?"

Jacinta smirked as she fed Mina's own line back to her. "I'm not."

"Being punished is going to be ten times worse if we're all mad at each other," Kelly pointed out. She nodded at Mina, trying to convince her to agree. "Mina, you're worried about Brian breaking up with you. That's all."

At the mention of Brian, Mina's eyes glossed over. She sagged like a rag doll then hugged her knees to her chest and retreated back into silence.

Kelly touched Jacinta's arm. "We know it wasn't an easy decision to get back with Raheem . . ."

"So does everybody think I'm dumb for going back with him?" Jacinta asked. Her eyes blazed first at Kelly then at Lizzie.

Lizzie's mouth opened then closed, then opened once more before she gave up and looked at Kelly.

Kelly's eyebrows hitched in a "thanks a lot" but she didn't miss a beat in answering, "You know him better than we do. It's your . . ."

"Kelly, either answer or I'm gonna take that bullshiggity as a yes," Jacinta warned, her eyebrows arched.

"Not dumb," Lizzie said, her tongue finally loosening. "I don't think you're dumb. But you know, I thought you were happier apart."

"I don't think you're dumb, either," Kelly said, offering no more. She shook her head. "That's me for believing Angel."

The awkward silence hung in the air until Mina spoke up. "I already said I didn't think you were dumb." She shrugged. "But if a dude hits you 'cause he's all pissed then you go back with him, what's gonna stop him from doing it again?"

Jacinta turned toward the mirror, as if rejecting Mina's sentiments. She plucked with her hair, watching her friends in the mirror. They watched her watching them, the silence thickening once more.

"Real talk . . . y'all can be mad at me if you want." Jacinta turned back around. She sat atop the dresser. Her voice had lost its angry edge. "But we're friends, right?" She looked each one of the girls in the eye and waited for them to nod or say yes before continuing. "I respect that y'all watching out for me. But what goes down between me and Heem is our business."

Her eyes lingered on Mina. An understanding that they weren't very different at all hung in the air between them. She stopped talking and for a second the only sound was the hum of the heating unit. Right on cue, it hissed and cut itself off as Jacinta spoke again. "Mina, Jessica is two-faced. She always will be. She doesn't like you." Jacinta waited for Mina to look back at her. When she did, she continued tenderly. "You my girl and I got your back. But I'm not gonna keep battling her for you."

"I didn't ask you to," Mina said, resigned.

Jacinta's eyes brightened with assurance as she said, "But you know if I had been there tonight I would have been down for whatever."

Mina nodded.

"Still, if you gonna put yourself out there to let her dog you . . ."

Jacinta shook her head, letting Mina fill in the blanks. A soft whoosh of air streamed from her nose, as if the effort to purge herself of her honest thoughts was a burden. She looked at Kelly and Mina and Lizzie's eyes automatically shifted, too. "I was never really down for you and Angel. Y'all too different."

Kelly tucked at her hair, but held Jacinta's gaze.

"The bad part is, I think he really does like you." Jacinta snorted. "But either you gonna like him the way he is or you gotta dip. And I'm cool with whatever. You know?"

"Well, we're done," Kelly said. Seeing the doubt in her friends' eyes, she added quickly. "No, seriously."

Jacinta looked at Lizzie and put up her hands as if to say, *I don't know about you.* She chuckled. "Lizzie, I'm seriously thinking of trying some of that seventeeth century, taking it slow courting stuff. You're the only sane one in our sad little bunch."

"You know, I was thinking the same thing," Lizzie said. She fell to the floor giggling as Mina booted her off the bed.

The uneasy shared chuckle grew to a more assured, genuine laugh. Soon the girls let their own troubles give way to Lizzie's happier tale, content to listen to her talk about her and Todd's long walk on the beach.

They allowed her drowsy chatter about Todd's easygoing humor to renew hope that their thorny run-ins with love were temporary. They wished upon her description of a tender kiss that tomorrow would put a brighter spin on their cracked, broken and bruised relationships.

No one chastised Jacinta when Raheem eventually called and she slid into the bathroom for privacy.

They all gave Kelly a silent "big ups" when she ignored Angel's repeated calls and text messages.

And they quickly let Mina off the hook, convincing her it totally wasn't desperate when she sent Brian several text messages asking if they could talk. If they thought she was desperate, no one held it against her. And if they noticed that she fell asleep, cell phone to her chest in a prayer-like clutch, no one let on.

Before they nodded out, piled haphazardly across one another in the same bed, they'd made up, the bickering behind them, their anger exhausted.

The morning would bring reality back, swift and in their face.

Having one another was good, because it would be all they'd have for at least four weeks. They were going to be punished for road tripping, for sure.

That they knew.

What they didn't know was that by this time next year, from fresh fish to silly sophomores, one of them would battle a cloying desire and lose.

And one would task herself with saving them all from themselves.

THAT'S WHAT'S UP!

A Del Rio Bay Novel

PAULA CHASE

ABOUT THIS GUIDE

The following questions are intended to
enhance your group's reading of
THAT'S WHAT'S UP!
by Paula Chase

DISCUSSION QUESTIONS

1. Jessica openly dislikes Mina. Would you rather have someone be open about how they feel about you, like Jessica? Or have someone who pretends to like you to your face, but does and says the opposite about you to others behind your back? Which one, and why?

2. Do you think Jacinta sent Raheem mixed messages by still hooking up with him even though they were broken up? Do actions speak louder than words?

3. If you were Jacinta, what would you do to move on with your life after a breakup, even if you still have to see the person regularly?

4. Was it fair for Kelly to expect Angel to change for her? If he had changed, did Kelly "owe" him anything for him making such a significant change in his lifestyle?

5. Mina is a self-proclaimed "drama magnet" but what, if anything, could she have done to avoid drama this go-round?

6. The clique often draws strength from one another, which explains why Lizzie was talked into road tripping without permission. Is there a difference between peer pressure and feeling safety among your close circle of friends? If so, what is it?

7. Do you think Mina and Brian broke up at the end? If a guy you were dating were caught in a compromising position, like Mina was in the picture kissing Craig, would you forgive him? Why or why not?

8. Mina is angry that Jacinta forgives Raheem for slapping her. Role Play: With one person playing Mina's part, talk to your friend about why being with someone who hits you is wrong. Another person play Jacinta and explain why you would give someone a second chance after such a foul act.

9. Can you break up with a guy and still be friends? Why or why not?

10. Should you try? Or should a breakup mean no contact, no friendship, no nothing?

For more information about domestic abuse among teens, visit the **Just About Teens** section of www.loveisnotabuse.com.

Stay tuned for the next book in this series:
WHO YOU WIT'?
Available in November 2008 wherever books are sold.
Until then, satisfy your Del Rio Bay craving
with the following excerpt from the next installment.

ENJOY!

The Fifteen-Minute Make-Out

"I hate how much I love you so."
—Rihanna ft. Ne-Yo, "Hate That I Love You"

*I*t *feels too good.*
It feels too good.
It feels too good.

Lizzie chanted to herself to break the spell of the warm frenzy building between her and Todd as he nibbled at her ear, stroked her side with one hand and pulled her flush against him with the other. Her breath hitched. Every time she attempted to move an inch or say something to slow the rush, he'd do something magical with his fingers or lips, hushing her.

She tried again, managing to move her head an inch.

Victory.

She parted her lips to say something (anything) and Todd's lips moved to hers. She instinctively kissed him back, rolling the icy cool taste of Orbit spearmint around her tongue, savoring it. It was hard to chew gum, now, without thinking of Todd and flushing.

As a matter of fact, it was hard to do a lot of things without thinking of Todd.

The realization struck her dumb.

No matter how hard she tried, it was hard to connect that practical, straight A, theater geek *her* not only had a serious boyfriend, but a popular, honest-to-goodness hot guy.

Six-foot-one, blue eyes, unruly light walnut-y hair highlighted blond, and ready with a joke the second he opened his mouth, Todd had a hot surfer dude look going. Truth be told, even when he let the blond grow out, he was easy on the eyes. He was also a full member of Club six-pack. And his biceps and chest weren't bad either. If Lizzie hadn't seen his body change with her own eyes, she would have never believed someone could go from skinny to sculpted in two years.

Yet, it still took her by surprise when girls went out of their way to flirt with him or give her nasty looks when she and Todd walked down the hall together. To her, he was still the goofy, skinny "T" who used to shadow JZ like a puppy when they were ten years old. Because of that and their existing middle school friendship, she and Todd were a comfortable couple. She never felt self-conscious around him, because whenever her nerves would attempt a takeover, like worrying that she had food stuck in her teeth and had to get it off before he saw it, Todd would poke fun at it, reminding her that he didn't care about her being the perfect girl.

Everyone seemed to know Todd was hot, except Todd.

That made it easy to get caught up in his charm.

Except . . . Lizzie wasn't ready to be completely ga-ga.

She was changing and some of the changes felt good. Really good, in fact.

But mostly they were unsettling. Like now. Why couldn't she open her mouth to say, "Hey, let's take a break"?

How come her brain was directing her body to move, get up, put some space between her and Todd, and it wouldn't obey?

Todd was becoming a priority in ways Lizzie had always secretly claimed no guy ever would.

Flubbing lines in theater when he popped into her mind. Getting a "B" on her chem test after their first real argument. She didn't recognize herself sometimes.

But things were about to take a turn, if all went according to plan.

Todd's kisses rained down on her in quick pecks. She met his lips with her own slow, but firm kisses, encouraging him to gel with her, easing him back a little until their kissing was in sync. Her resolve melted. It always did around the twelve-minute make-out mark. Instead of panicking that things were going too far, Lizzie gave in, savoring Todd's warm breath on her neck, ears, then his lips on hers.

Step one of her plan would kick in, in exactly five . . .

Todd's tongue darted in her mouth for a quick visit then was gone.

Four . . .

His hands pushed her shirt up just enough so Lizzie could feel their coolness on her warm belly.

Three . . .

He stroked her waist, careful not to go near her armpit (he'd learned the hard way that she'd burst into a fit of giggles, busting up the mood) but working closer to her bra.

Two . . .

Lizzie inhaled sharply as his hands made soft, smooth circles on her belly.

One . . .

Todd's fingers were on the front clasp of her bra just as Lizzie's cell phone blared "One" from *A Chorus Line* filling the room with a choral-like, "One, singular sensation, every little step he takes."

Todd hesitated for a fleeting second.

Lizzie pushed herself upright. Her chest heaved as she ran her fingers through her tousled hair.

Todd's eyes, wide with surprise, skated from Lizzie to the phone in confusion.

Lizzie kneeled against the sofa, picked the phone up and turned off the alarm she'd set right before she and Todd began making out. She was getting so good at doing it, fingers flying to set it before the kissing began, he never noticed. Smiling, she dipped her head and bunched her cascade of blonde hair into a quick and dirty ponytail before standing up. She put her hand out to help Todd up from the floor.

His long body unfolded into a standing position where he towered a full foot over Lizzie.

"Dude, I hate your phone." Todd shook his head, eyeing the phone with disdain. "It rings every time we . . ." He dropped down onto the sofa, dramatically pouting.

Lizzie pretended to check the missed call, even though there was none. "It's Mina. JZ should be here any minute to get us," she practically sang, giddy that once more her fifteen-minute make-out alarm had done its job.

Todd ran his fingers through his unruly locks, gathering himself. He looked shell-shocked and Lizzie almost felt sorry for him.

Almost.

She felt (a little) bad for having to trick him, but she couldn't trust herself anymore to untangle herself from the increasingly hot and heavy make-outs. At some point, they were going to stop working. Either Todd was going to throw her phone out the window—he was eyeing it now like he wanted to—or simply not let her jump up like someone had lit her pants on fire, to check it.

She knew the day was coming. That's why it was time for the virginity pact.

Satisfied with herself, she plopped down beside Todd.

"I'm starved. You?"

"Yeah, but not for pizza," Todd said, making googly eyes at her.

Lizzie planted a prim peck on his lips, allowing it to turn into a bit more before pulling away. Todd reached out to pull her back, but Lizzie was up in a flash, laughing as his hand swiped her T-shirt, catching only air.

He scowled, chiding her playfully. "Tease."

"Sucker." She sprinted clumsily as he chased her up the stairs.

The doorbell rang as they reached the landing.

She hadn't planned it, but the cavalry had arrived right on time.

HAVEN'T HAD ENOUGH?
CHECK OUT THESE OTHER GREAT SERIES
FROM DAFINA BOOKS!

DRAMA HIGH
by L. Divine
Follow the adventures of a young sistah who's learning life in the 'hood is nothing compared to life in high school.

THE FIGHT	SECOND CHANCE	AYD'S LEGACY
ISBN: 0-7582-1633-5	ISBN: 0-7582-1635-1	ISBN: 0-7582-1637-8

FRENEMIES	LADY J
ISBN: 0-7582-2532-6	ISBN: 0-7582-2534-2

BOY SHOPPING
by Nia Stephens
An exciting "you pick the ending" series that lets the reader pick Mr. Right.

BOY SHOPPING	LIKE THIS AND LIKE THAT	GET MORE
ISBN: 0-7582-1929-6	ISBN: 0-7582-1931-8	ISBN:0-7582-1933-4

DEL RIO BAY
by Paula Chase
A wickedly funny series that explores friendship, betrayal, and how far some people will go for popularity.

SO NOT THE DRAMA	DON'T GET IT TWISTED
ISBN: 0-7582-1859-1	ISBN: 0-7582-1861-3

PERRY SKKY JR.
by Stephanie Perry Moore
An inspirational series that follows the adventures of a high school football star as he balances faith and the temptations of teen life.

PRIME CHOICE	PRESSING HARD	PROBLEM SOLVED
ISBN: 0-7582-1863-X	ISBN: 0-7582-1872-9	SBN: 0-7582-1874-5

PRAYED UP
ISBN: 0-7582-2538-5